SURRENDER

SURRENDER

EROTIC TALES OF
FEMALE PLEASURE AND SUBMISSION

EDITED BY
RACHEL KRAMER BUSSEL

Published in the United States by Cleis Press, Inc.,
2246 Sixth Street, Berkeley, California 94710.

Printed in the United States.
Cover design: Scott Idleman/Blink
Cover photograph: Barbara Nitke
Text design: Frank Wiedemann
Cleis Press logo art: Juana Alicia
First Edition.
10 9 8 7 6 5 4 3 2 1

ISBN: 978-1-57344-652-5

Permissions appear on page 226.

Contents

INTRODUCTION: SURRENDERING TO PLEASURE— AND POWER

I'm not surprised to learn that female submission is a hot topic. For the many women who fantasize about giving up control, bending over, hearing the click of a pair of handcuffs, or engaging in kinky role-play, that desire can consume them—and lead them to some wicked fantasies.

The stories here run the gamut, from couples engaged in hardcore kink to the psychology of submission, with everything from coming in public to submitting to a Krav Maga teacher.

Whether you know you're a submissive (sometimes or all the time, or just in your head) or you're simply curious, this book provides an opportunity to read about things you might want to try, some you'd never dare, and some that will likely stay in your mind (and other body parts) for a long time to come. For me, the best erotica not only arouses my senses and my libido, but takes me all the way into the character who's experiencing such deliciously exciting erotic encounters. It teaches me about myself and about what gets other people off. It gives me fodder to bring back to the bedroom and makes me surrender to its heated words.

These encounters are mostly focused on the women, the brats, the subs, the bad girls, but in them, you will find the most wicked of tops—wickedly insightful, wickedly mean, wickedly sadistic, wickedly keen on prompting pleasure out of these women who have chosen them to surrender to. These are the men who know the right time to push a woman's buttons—and boundaries—to concoct vivid experiments in kink. Some of these tales are from their point of view, offering insight into what it's like to desire a woman, to be bound and at their mercy.

I shouldn't have to say this, but I feel I must: these stories are not about men violating women. They are not about women being abused or mistreated. They are about women accessing a side of themselves that many of us bury, precisely because we feel it's not "feminist" enough or is somehow otherwise politically incorrect to want to kneel, bend over, open our mouths, spread our legs, submit, and surrender. As Dominic says in "Power Over Power" to his student, Jackie: "You're looking for power. In your own way, getting fucked rough like that will make you feel powerful. Is that right?" Vince echoes this to his wife in "Veronica's Body," when he instructs her, "Don't ever back down from me." He wants a woman who can meet him in bed as an equal partner even as he whips her until she trembles. When he disciplines her, it's an act of love as much as, if not more than, an act of kinkiness.

Good BDSM erotica makes you understand all the emotions that can come into play when, well, playing: there can be uncertainty, nervousness, fear, excitement. I selected each of the 22 stories in *Surrender* because they're blazingly hot and because they illuminate some aspect of submission that I think is important.

The authors of the stories you're about to read understand

the art of submission and the thrill of surrender, whether that is personal space, sight ("Without Eyes" by Terri Pray) or culinary choices ("Lunch" by Elizabeth Coldwell). What the women here want is to give up part of themselves to gain something else. They may still be skittish, but overcoming their fears, surrendering to them, yields beauty, pleasure and, in its own way, power.

In the very creative opener by Donna George Storey, "Dear Professor Pervert," a student learns several very kinky lessons about how to get off—and follow orders. With "Daddy's Girl," Teresa Noelle Roberts takes the topic of Daddy/girl play (which, I fully confess, is not something I normally enjoy reading) and turns it into a kinky role-playing tale that stays hot throughout while also explaining the Daddy dynamic. Emerald delivers a riveting tale of power play in "Power Over Power," where a Krav Maga instructor shows his student that the heart of her true power lies in her owning her submission and baring more than just her body.

In "The Chair" by Lolita Lopez, the title object becomes the ultimate sex toy for Cal to use in teasing and tormenting Lily, while Susan in Terri Pray's "Without Eyes" goes from being irate to being on her knees in moments.

Anticipation is often the hottest part of a scene, with the sub wondering when and how the action will happen. In "The Hardest Part," Alison Tyler offers up the exquisite torture of waiting for your kinky fantasies to come true:

> *I'm over his lap. I've been needing a spanking for too long, and he's been making me wait. In spite of everything I've done, he's ignored the signals. I've been bratty. I've been bad. I may as well have worn a t-shirt with the words SPANK ME in bold scarlet letters across the front.*

In "Rapunzel" by Jacqueline Applebee, when a woman agrees to give up her long locks, she bares herself in an unexpected way (any woman who's ever submitted to a hairdresser's chair knows the tension and masochism involved!), while in "The Royalton-A Daray Tale," Tess Danesi makes a blindfold fantasy come true in an upscale hotel.

With "The Sun is an Ordinary Story," Shanna Germain takes something you wouldn't expect to read about in an erotica book—cancer—and offers up a vitally human story about the transformative power of kink and how getting back to playing rough makes one woman feel more alive than ever.

In my story "Belted," the narrator wonders what it is about her lover that turns her on quite so much:

> *Is it the belt that makes you come? The leather, the thrash, the pain, the jolt? Is it the force behind it? Is it the noises he makes as he does it, the hitches of breath that are nothing like your shuddering sobs but are music to your ears nonetheless—is that what makes you finally go over the edge? Is it him holding you down, him promising you pain that may or may not come?*

I love stories that delve into the psychology of BDSM, and few writers do that better than Elizabeth Coldwell. With "Lunch," she will not only have you eyeing your fellow deli customers with a keener eye, but also show you the erotic potential within even the smallest decisions, once you've given up the decision-making power to someone else.

Erotica impresario Thomas S. Roche gives us "Schoolgirl and Angel," in which a top and his sub find a new plaything at a dungeon party, one who's a little more mouthy than they're used to. Serena winds up taking off her panties in public, among many other things, in Teresa Noelle Roberts' "First Date with the Dom." With "In Control," online negotiation between SLUTSLAVE and her master turns to him using chopsticks to tweak her sensitive nipples before moving on to heavier equipment. Author M. Christian captures the silent but powerful interplay between top and bottom, those moments that say more than sometimes words ever can: "She lifted her head, looking long at me, breathing heavy and hard. Her eyes flicked with a bit of fear but more than anything, a kind of plea: *More.*"

Sometimes a bratty girl doesn't even know she's begging to be put in her place, or how much she might like someone else taking control. In "Wild Child" by Matt Conklin, an older man sees beneath the veneer of the young woman sitting next to him on a plane, all too happy to show her what true rebellion is all about. In "Brianna's Fire" by Amanda Earl, a slave is put to the test, while "Forceful Personalities" come into play in Dominic Santi's contribution when Christa takes a while to submit, even though she wants to desperately. That tension between wanting to be as slutty as we are in our fantasies, and actually doing it, plays out in numerous other stories as well. In the aforementioned "Veronica's Body" by Isabelle Gray, a husband and wife manage to leave behind their everyday personae in order to communicate on a more intense level, one that deepens their marriage as she lets him use her, both of them getting off on the experience. Sightseeing isn't just for those wearing fanny packs! A tourist attraction provides a welcome opportunity for public sex in Justine Elyot's "The London O."

In Fiona Locke's "Pink Cheeks," a woman who's been lurking in another online forum finds out what happens when someone she sees every day finds out her naughtiest secrets. Finally, in Gwen Masters' "How Bad Do You Want It?" she asks the title question, which I might turn over to you, dear reader. I have a feeling you want it very, very badly, "it" being all the most out-there, I-could-never (yet I can't stop thinking about them) fantasies that flirt at the edges of your mind when you are getting yourself off, alone or with a partner.

I invite you to surrender to these stories, whether they make you blush or squirm, whether they make you curious, wet, excited, or even a little uneasy. I want these stories to show you the range of ways a woman can surrender, and prove that us submissive women are in no way shrinking wallflowers. We are sexy precisely because we have the strength to say "yes" to the "degrading" thoughts that float through our minds and power our orgasms.

Rachel Kramer Bussel
New York City

DEAR PROFESSOR PERVERT

Donna George Storey

Assignment #4: Bring yourself to orgasm without using your fingers, hands, vibrator or other sex toy. Record the experience in your Masturbation Journal, following the usual guidelines. Your last submission showed much improvement—the use of imagery and language was excellent. Keep up the good work. Sincerely, Professor Pervert.

I click CLOSE MAIL and smile. The professor probably thinks this one's going to be a challenge, but I already came up with the answer ten years ago—back when I was in college the first time around. Doing a "no-hands" is actually pretty easy. You bunch up your pillow, straddle it like a lover, and work your hips just so while you play with your nipples. It feels great, plus you get a good core workout.

Of course, I'll be required to confess that I'm bringing prior experience to the assignment, but I figure I can make up the lost points with an extrasteamy journal entry. I was pretty inhibited at the beginning, but the professor's right. I am improving.

I stroll over to the linen closet and take out a towel. Today I have about two hours to complete the assignment and write it up. If I don't have my paper in his inbox by 9:00 p.m. London time, there will be "penalties." Afterward I'll have just enough time to shower and get to campus for my real summer school class, The Twentieth Century British Novel.

I pull off my oversized T-shirt and shimmy out of my panties. *Totally naked, above and below.* That's what I'll write under *What were you wearing?* in the journal.

Next I fold the pillow and wrap it in the towel. I always get very juicy when I'm doing it for the professor. I stretch out on the bed and push the pillow between my legs, resting on my elbows to allow for good access to my breasts, which *dangle like cones of white wisteria, tinted tender pink at the tips.* The professor will love that. He specializes in the Romantic poets and is partial to natural imagery.

I note the time on the clock above my bed, then cross my arms and begin to caress my breasts, my right hand cupping the left tit, my left hand stroking the right. My nipples feel soft and satiny and more sensitive than when I'm lying on my back, my usual position for self-pleasuring. I push my hips into the pillow, grimacing at the nubby texture of the towel against my tender slit. Maybe this isn't the answer after all?

Think, Tina, think. The rest will come.

It's the professor's voice, smooth and deep, guiding me ever onward to new achievements.

I close my eyes and think.

A man steps from the melting red shadows behind my eyelids and stands at the bottom of my bed. His gaze is fixed on my naked ass. I can feel it, as bright and hot as a spotlight. I squirm involuntarily and that sweet, achy sensation of longing floods my belly. What is he thinking and feeling as he watches a horny slut masturbate just for him?

I begin to hump the pillow with slow, rhythmic thrusts. I can make out the man's face more clearly now—the lush, curly brown hair, the wire-rim Russian Revolutionary glasses. He is young—only two years older than I am and not even tenured yet—but he has enough of a snotty academic air that I yearn to rub away at that smug composure with every jerk of my hips. I want him so jealous of this pillow that he'll start begging me to let him take its place between my legs.

I pause mid-thrust and sigh. The sensation still isn't intense enough to bring me off. It might work if I could use my fingers to spread my labia and get direct friction on my clit, but of course, the assignment specifically forbids it.

I know you have it in you, Tina. Push a little harder. Show me how naughty you are deep inside.

"Yes, Professor," I whisper, into the air. I do want him to see me; not just my flesh, but my darker, deeper places.

The room shifts; the morning light filtering through the curtains turns to a harsh fluorescent buzz. Steel prison bars bisect the room, and my bed becomes a cot covered with a rough, gray blanket. I'm still humping a pillow, my bare buttocks aimed straight at the bars, but the audience has expanded tenfold. A carefully selected squad of prisoners has been brought here to watch an oversexed girl get herself off without using her hands. It's not clear if this is a reward or a punishment for these hardened criminals. I know the guards are sadists. They've told me that if I don't come this way in twenty minutes, the whole crew of correctional officers will get to fuck me on the sagging sofa in their employee lounge in ascending order of cock size. They warned me with a leer that the biggest one, Harry the

Horse, has a dick that would put a baseball bat to shame.

The stakes are definitely higher now.

I rock my hips faster against the damp towel. The prisoners' eyes bore into my flesh. They're bad guys, lifers. They haven't had a woman in decades, and their soft howls of frustration ricochet off the concrete walls. With a fearful glance over my shoulder, I see their huge, swollen cocks are protruding from their flies. Some pump themselves frantically, heedless of the grinning guard. One pushes himself through the bars, fucking the air, as if he can enter me that way if he tries hard enough.

"Boys, you've got five minutes to finish your business, then it's back to your cells," the guard barks. Then his voice turns to sugar with a touch of poison. "You, too, sweetheart. Five minutes or you know what we've got waiting for you."

"I've seen enough assholes in this joint. Make her flip over and show us her cunt," a hoarse voice grumbles.

I hear the crack of a fist landing on flesh, a bellow of pain.

"What you see is what you get," the guard growls.

The men moan and grunt like beasts as they hurry to empty their balls. My head is bursting with lewd sounds, the rasp of dick flesh being rubbed in spit-moistened fists, the rhythmic knocking of hips against the bars that keep me cruelly out of their reach.

One man stands back, eyes narrowed, arms crossed, his fly firmly zipped. He is watching me, but he's also watching them watching me. It's the professor. Even in this place, as far away from twining ivy as you can get, he's still the one in control.

My nipples are as hard as little pebbles now. When I flick them with my fingers, electric jolts jump straight to my pussy. I'm gyrating like a stripper, sliding my cunt down over the pillow, then jerking back up, like my ass is tethered to a spring. Though I'm usually quiet when I masturbate, I realize I'm making sounds, too: deep grunts and harsh bellows to harmonize with the *bang-bang* of the headboard against the wall. But I'm going to make it in time. I can feel the orgasm begin to grow, a throbbing knot in my gut. And the prisoners are right there with me. With a collective groan, they shoot their wads through the bars, spraying my ass with a sizzling fountain of spunk. The odor fills my nostrils, hay mixed with something harsh and tinny; the nastiest, naughtiest smell on earth. It's all I need to push me over the edge. I ride the pillow like a bucking bronco, screaming myself hoarse as I climax, each contraction harder and sweeter than ever before.

As the spasms fade to a flutter, I check the clock. Length of session: twenty minutes from start to finish. I collapse facedown on the bed and listen to my pounding heart. So far, so good, but this is just the beginning. It's never really over until the professor gives me my grade.

"Isn't that Professor Perkins over there? And you've got his table, Tina. Lucky bitch."

Pam and I had a lot in common. We were both education majors with a minor in English lit; we both worked weekends at Chez Jacqueline. Of course, she was twenty-one. I was eight years older and far too worldly-wise to gush over an attractive young assistant professor.

"Those must be his parents," I said, eyeing the other members of his party: a slim, well-dressed older woman and a gray-haired guy who looked more or less like the professor with thirty years on him. Chez Jackie's was the best restaurant in town and we often waited on our teachers and their families. I was curious to see how Perkins would act when he was off duty. In class he was affable but no-nonsense—forget about getting an extension on a paper from him.

To my surprise he was positively charming in the candlelit glow of the dining room. He remembered my name and introduced me to his folks with a jaunty, "Tina's without question my best student this semester."

"I know Pam gave you a free dessert when you said that to her last week, Professor, but I'm a tougher nut to crack." I grinned at his dad, who winked back.

"Damn. Because this time it's actually true," Professor Perkins joined right in.

Mom smiled, too, and did a little back-and-forth glance between her son and me that made it clear the professor wasn't currently attached, but Mom was hoping he might find a nice girl soon and she might possibly be yours truly. Which almost made me laugh out loud because I was far too busy getting my life back together to waste time lusting after my professor. Okay, so I did occasionally let my mind wander during class. I'd picture the professor naked and try to guess what his cock looked like erect. Long and slender or thick and florid? Ramrod straight or curved to the left as any P.C. professor's should be? Once or twice I even imagined what it would be like to ride him and watch his face as he came. But I did that with every professor, including the old silver-beards and—during really boring lectures—even a few of the women.

But I should've remembered that Mom always knows best.

I was heading back to the kitchen with a tray of dirty plates when Professor Perkins stepped out of the hallway by the restrooms.

"Excuse me, I know you're busy," he stammered. "But I wanted to let you know I turned in the final grades for your class yesterday."

My stomach did a somersault. Why would he look so nervous unless he had bad news? Yet I'd gotten an *A* on the midterm and very complimentary comments on the final paper: *Your argument is tight and compelling, the writing smooth and flowing—a true pleasure to read.*

The professor smiled as if he read my thoughts. "Don't worry, you did very well. I mentioned it because I'm now ethically allowed to ask if you'd like to get together for coffee or something."

Could it be that while I was fantasizing about Professor Perkins naked, he was returning the favor? Maybe I'd get to see what his cock looked like after all.

"Thanks, Professor. Actually, a bunch of us usually go over to the tapas place for a drink after work around eleven. You're welcome to join us tonight—if your mom and dad give you permission."

He blushed—I was starting to like this shy suitor side of him—but recovered quickly and gave me a grin. "I'm sure I can talk them into relaxing my curfew tonight. After all, there's no school tomorrow. See you later, then, Tina."

I had to admit I felt a little thrill as I watched him stride back to his doting parents. Professor Perkins had me in his power all semester. Now I was turning the tables.

Or so I thought.

Assignment #5: Go to the woman-friendly adult store south of campus. Ask a saleswoman for advice on anal toys. Confess your level of experience—beginner, dabbler, veteran ready for a challenge? Purchase the item she recommends as well as a bottle of lubricant. When you return home, insert the toy in your anus and masturbate. Record the experience in your Masturbation Journal, following the usual guidelines. Your last assignment earned A for the journal entry, which was nicely paced with evocative imagery. However, I gave you a B- for practical execution. The point of these exercises is for you to attempt something you haven't tried before. I expect you to obey this rule in the future. If you accumulate enough demerits, it will be necessary to discipline you appropriately. Sincerely, Professor Pervert.

Ah, yes, Assignment #5. That's why I'm here in this strange pose: sitting on my bed with my back against the headboard, my legs spread wide. It's the only position that lets me keep the butt plug in place while I diddle myself.

Naturally, I bought the beginner's size, a flesh-colored silicone gadget about the size of my ring finger with a bulge in the middle like a swollen knuckle. The bottom flares out into a rectangular base to keep the device from slipping all the way inside. That's what the butch-looking saleswoman at the sex store explained to me. Fortunately, buying the thing was not as embarrassing as I had feared. The woman was so nonchalant, it was like we were discussing lipstick instead of anal sex toys. That is, except at the very end when she handed me the brown paper bag and said, "Enjoy!" with a big grin as if she could see exactly what I'd be doing with my purchase before the afternoon was through. I blushed beet red and rushed out of the store.

To be honest, I probably do make as lewd a picture as anyone could imagine. I'm dressed in the scarlet waist cincher and thigh-highs I bought for Assignment #3, which only accentuate all the bare, juicy parts of me. The air brushes my exposed pussy like cool fingertips, and my nipples are standing out stiff and red. Yet I can't say I'm all that turned on by the assignment so far. For one thing, I'm not sure I bought the right size plug. It was definitely a challenge pushing it inside me—I was poking the slippery, lubed-up thing around my butt crack for a full min-ute—but now that it's there, I can hardly feel it. I'm more excited by the idea that I did this naughty thing just for the professor.

Not that he's here to see me. Yet.

I close my eyes and take a deep breath. Suddenly the summer sunlight fades to a single green-shaded lamp glowing in the au-tumn dusk. I'm sitting on a leather sofa in the same slutty getup, legs open, asshole impaled on a strange little silicone bowling pin. Across from me sits the professor in a wingback chair, flanked by tall bookcases jammed with erudite tomes. With his eyes alone he issues the command: *Touch yourself, Tina. For me.*

My hand dips between my legs. I start to strum. My finger makes a rude clicking sound in the wet folds, and I blush, know-ing he hears and sees it all.

"Are you enjoying this?" he asks, his voice as soft as a silk scarf trailing over naked flesh.

"Yes, Professor," I admit shyly.

"Just 'yes?' That's a vague answer," he snaps. "I want you to be specific about what you find enjoyable. Is it that X-rated toy you shoved up your ass so greedily or the fact that I'm watching you masturbate?"

My throat constricts with shame, but I manage to croak out an answer. "Both, Professor."

"Indeed? I must say I'm enjoying myself as well. But I think we're both disappointed you bought the small one. Next time I want you to get one of the long, fat monsters that made you cringe when you saw them on the shelf. While you're at it, get yourself a big dildo—with veins and a suction cup that sticks to a chair so you can ride it. And another one for your mouth, too. You'd like that, wouldn't you, to be all filled up in every empty, aching hole?"

"Yes, Professor," I whisper. That's the only answer I can ever give him, but in truth I'm not sure I agree. No plastic cock—no matter how huge or swollen—can satisfy me as well as his hot, probing gaze.

"Shall I send you back to the store right now to tell that dyke you're enjoying your timid little butt plug very much, thank you, but you crave something bigger and nastier?"

My heart leaps in my chest. "No, please. I'll do anything for you here in your office, but please don't make me do that, Professor."

He laughs softly. "Your cunt muscles contract very nicely when you're frightened. Which gives me an idea for something we can do here to remedy the situation. At my command, I want you to squeeze your muscles around the toy as tightly as you can and hold it until I tell you to release. Will you do that for me?"

"Yes, Professor," I gasp, my buttocks slipping on the leather of the sofa, already slick with my sweat and juices.

"All right then. Squeeze."

I clutch the butt plug, panting softly. I'm starting to ache back there, but the professor only watches me squirm, silently, for what seems like an eternity. Finally he deigns to utter the words I'm desperate to hear.

"You may release."

I breathe out. An intense tingling sensation radiates from my asshole, up through my torso, and down through my shivering thighs. My jaw drops open and I utter an involuntary moan of pleasure.

"Spread your legs a little wider," he orders coolly. "It makes your pussy lips push out so I can see your hole. You're so slick and swollen today, Tina. I think anal play agrees with you. Once more now, squeeze…"

I grip the toy again, gritting my teeth.

"…and release."

The professor is definitely onto something. My asshole's on fire, the flames shooting higher, licking at my throbbing clit. My finger dances over my stiff little girl-cock sticking out shamelessly, all hard and hungry for the professor to see. I'm going to make it. I'm going to come in front of him with this obscene rubber toy jammed up my ass.

"May I...have...an orgasm, Professor?" I'm too distracted by the sensations to remember if this was part of the assignment.

"Of course, Tina, I always like to see my students bring their work to a satisfying conclusion. I would indeed like you to come—but only at the precise moment I give the order. Is that understood?"

"Yes, Professor." I obediently slow my clit finger to coasting speed. But will my cunt submit as easily to his command?

"Come for me, Tina," he tells me. "Now."

With a grunt, I attack my clit with frantic jabs and squeeze the toy with all my might and—oh, God, it's happening—a wave of burning heat fans through my belly, erupting from my throat in a series of barking cries, as my back bangs against the headboard and my anus milks the butt plug in helpless, rhythmic spasms.

When it's over, I slide down onto the bed and pop the toy out, wrapping it in a waiting tissue. Total time for the session: thirty-five minutes. In my journal entry, I'll tell the professor about his "help" of course, but I'm not sure words will do justice to the quality of my orgasm—a detailed description of which is a strict requirement for each assignment. It was definitely different. It seemed to start deeper inside me, a secret explosion tucked back against my spine. Yet there was something else I couldn't quite name, a hint of exotic spice in a familiar sweet. The only way I can really be sure I'll get a good grade is to try it again and take more careful notes.

I laugh to myself. Strange how my lover is thousands of miles away, but I'm having more and better sex than I've ever had in my life.

After our first "date" for drinks, things moved fast with Professor Perkins. After all, I'd already met his parents. Within the week, I saw his cock, too. It was average in length, but thick, and it turned a lovely rosy color when it got hard that made me think of a strawberry Popsicle, my favorite flavor.

Professor Perkins—I was calling him Jonathan by then—was pretty good in bed, too. At first he was slow and careful, as if he were studying my body to get an *A* in Tina's Sexual Response 101. But soon enough we were rutting like wild animals. After the sex, we had some pretty intense talks, too. Jonathan told me about his romance with a colleague that didn't survive when she left him for a job on the East Coast. I told him why I dropped out of college the first time: to follow my boyfriend, Devon, on his pilgrimage around the world. Our first year together was the most magical year of my life. The next five were the worst. It was all about Devon's drinking until one day I realized I was giving my life to a man who didn't know me, who didn't even see me at all.

"I love to look at you," Jonathan said, stroking my hair. "And I want to know everything about you."

He was certainly saying and doing all the right things. In fact, it all seemed too good to be true. It was. A minute later, Jonathan told me he was leaving for London the following Monday to do research at the British Library and would be gone for six weeks.

Okay, a few dates and a few fucks didn't really give me any claim on him, but I felt deserted by the bastard all the same.

Still the first week apart wasn't so bad. We emailed every day and Jonathan hinted during a Skype call that he'd love to take me hiking around Wordsworth's Dove Cottage in the Lake

Country—next summer perhaps. Could a guy get more sweet and Romantic than that?

In fact, it was my dirty mind that led us down a darker, more twisted trail. It all started innocently enough with a naughty dream.

I was lying on the floor of Professor Perkins' office wearing an old-fashioned schoolgirl's kilt and white blouse. The professor himself was stretched out on top of me, but he didn't really have a body. He was just a hot weight pressing me down, making my flesh feel all tingly and melted. I couldn't see his face either, but I felt his hand stroking my cheek and his voice slipping into my ear. *Your final paper was so good it made my cock hard for two weeks straight.*

Which, of course, didn't make any sense. I mean, how could a ten-page paper on "Ode on a Grecian Urn" give anyone a boner for one minute, not to mention two weeks? However, the dream got *me* so turned on, I lay in bed playing with myself and thinking about Jonathan until I had a very wet, loud orgasm. Even after that I was still horny and missing him terribly. That's how I got the idea to send him a provocative email.

In retrospect it was mild stuff. I told him about the dream and how I "pleasured myself" when I woke up. Then I said, tongue-in-cheek, that I was looking forward to August when I could feel his "pulsing manhood" in my "turgid sex."

After I sent it, I was a little worried he'd laugh or be offended, but instead he called and said in that low, syrupy voice guys get when they're shy but turned on at the same time, that he enjoyed my email and was going to send a reply soon.

I couldn't restrain a giggle of triumph. Last spring I never would have imagined I'd inspire Professor Perkins to send me an X-rated email.

But that wasn't quite what I got. The subject line was simply

Comments on Your Essay. In a formal, professor-ish tone, he told me my paper would be stronger if I gave more context for the self-pleasuring—what I was wearing, how long it took, and which specific techniques I used to reach satisfaction. He suggested I draw my reader into the scene through the use of vivid detail and avoid clichés such as "pulsing manhood." He concluded that my work showed promise, but there was much room for improvement.

My face burning with embarrassment and disbelief, I fired back a reply.

> *Dear Professor Pervert, I didn't realize I was going to be graded on my effort. Maybe you should write out the assignment with a list of guidelines so I can do better next time?*

A few hours later, I found this in my in-box:

> *Assignment #1: Spend at least an hour pleasuring yourself without bringing yourself to orgasm. After one hour, you may enjoy a climax. You'll be keeping a Masturbation Journal that will be graded on style and content. At the top of each entry record the time of day, length and location of session, and what you are (or are not) wearing as the session unfolds. I'm looking for an accurate and thoughtful essay that explores not only physical sensations, but your thoughts, feelings and fantasies while you are masturbating. Fresh images and honesty are key elements of the exercise. The assignment is due within four hours. Late papers will be penalized. Sincerely, Professor Pervert.*

"The nerve!" I sputtered at the computer, shaking with anger. For a minute, I was too worked up over his audacity to notice he'd gotten me worked up in other ways: my panties were soaking wet.

After I got an A for the butt plug scene, I was really looking forward to Assignment #6, but instead I received an email as terse as an old-fashioned telegram: *Coming home early, have to run to catch the flight. Can I see you Saturday afternoon? J.*

In spite of my excitement, I spent most of the morning worrying about what I'd say when I greeted him on my doorstep. "Hey, Professor Perkins, thanks again for reading my kinky fantasies about doing sex shows for convicts and sodomizing myself in your office"? Fortunately, conversation was low on our list of welcome home activities. The instant he arrived we were kissing and ripping off each other's clothes and, within about a minute, fucking like crazy.

Now we're twined together in the afterglow, and Jonathan is telling me how much he missed me and how I'm even more gorgeous than he remembered. Not that I don't like the adoration, but it's a bit cliché. Secretly I find myself missing another man, with more exacting standards, who has apparently decided to stay back in London.

As if he's read my thoughts, Jonathan clears his throat. "By the way, I, um, enjoyed your essays very much. I know it would be different in person, but I came up with some new ideas. It's totally cool with me if you'd rather not, but maybe some day we could…?"

My pulse jumps.

"Try Assignment Six?" I whisper.

He nods, blushing.

"I'd like that very much, Professor. In fact, I'd be up for a lesson right now."

His cock stirs against my thigh, and I feel a change in other parts of his body, too—a squaring of the shoulders, a confident lift to the chin. My heart is pounding now, with the power of it. Because I'm the one who's made this happen, with my words and my desire.

"Very well, Tina, I want you to get up and stand by the bed." His voice is slow and smooth, just as I imagined. "No, don't put on your robe, I want to look at you just as you are."

I crawl out of bed and stand before him. I can't meet his eyes, but I feel them, warm and glowing on my bare flesh. I've never felt so beautiful, so *seen*.

"You like to be watched doing naughty things, don't you, Tina? You like to do things no good girl would ever dream of."

"Yes, Professor," I whisper, my voice trembling.

"In fact, you want to masturbate for me right now, isn't that correct?"

"Yes, Professor." I slip an unsteady hand between my legs and start to rub my clit for him. Except this time he really is watching.

"Your reports were excellent, but I must say I'm enjoying the live performance. Now, for our next assignment I'll be asking you to do some new things that circumstances didn't allow before. I will push you, and stretch you, but I know you have it in you to get top grades."

I let out a soft moan. Images swirl through my head: my body bent over his desk in his office on campus, the professor behind me, probing my ass with the lubed-up knob of his dick. Me on my knees, hands bound behind my back as I suck and suck his strawberry Popsicle prick. I know there will be challenges, even humiliations, but any fear is lost in a sweet, soaring hunger to learn more about all the things our bodies and minds can do together.

"I'll try my best, Professor. If I may say so, sir, I'm glad you're back."

"All thanks to you, Tina. You are without question my most inspiring student. Now listen carefully to my instructions. As you know, I will take points off for sloppiness."

The only proper answer is to nod, obediently, but I can't help smiling, too. He is home, my dear Professor Pervert. I can't wait for class to begin.

DADDY'S GIRL

Teresa Noelle Roberts

Daddy strides into the living room, between me and the TV, and switches off the "Buffy" rerun I'm halfheartedly watching.

Then he holds up a pack of cigarettes and a romance novel. "I found these in your room, Cherise. What do you have to say for yourself?"

Heart pounding like a techno track, palms wet and mouth dry, I plaster on a brassy, totally fake smile. "You always tell me I should read more?"

I squeak at the end.

Damn it. He's caught me by surprise, and it's making me nervous.

"Smut isn't what I had in mind."

"It's just a romance novel, Daddy." I knew the cigarettes would get me in trouble, but I'm surprised he's harping on the book. He's always got his nose in a book—sometimes some classic, since he's a lit professor, but just as likely a thriller, and he knows I love a good romance as much as he loves a good save-the-world-from-the-bad-guys adventure.

Maybe the difference is that this is an *erotic* romance, and a kinky one at that?

I jump up and try to snatch the book away from him, but it's too late. He opens it at my bookmark, and begins to read out loud in a rich voice, like he's reading Shakespeare.

Oh, god. It's the part where the hero gives the heroine a sexy spanking. Hearing Daddy read it is so embarrassing.

Embarrassing, yet hot.

My face burns, and I squirm from humiliation and horniness, pressing my thighs closer together as if that would protect my clit from being attacked by lust.

Instead, it gets me excited.

It's not just what he's reading. What's getting to me is *him* reading it, with his deep whisky voice and the blue eyes behind the sexy-professor horn-rims, and the way he's disapproving and disdainful and amused all at once.

A girl's Daddy shouldn't read her things like that, in that way. It's just not what fathers do.

He's not playing by the rules, not following the script.

It's freaking me out and it's turning me on and it's freaking me out because it's turning me on.

He stops reading just as the characters move on from spanking to screwing. "What do you have to say for yourself, young woman? Doesn't that sound foolish, read aloud?" He's not just scolding me. He's making fun of me, too. Great.

I roll my eyes. "Daddy, it's just a book. I like it, and besides, Tom Clancy would sound just as dumb if I did a dramatic reading."

He takes a step forward, and then another, taking over my personal space. I'm surrounded by his cologne, the leathery-woodsy one that's like Essence of Grown Man, and I know I ought to back away, but instead I've grown roots into the rug.

"You're right about Tom Clancy," he admits. "But if you want to read about erotic spanking, let me find you something better. I doubt this author has been spanked since she was six years old and got caught stealing cookies."

God, what am I supposed to say to that? He's so not playing by the rules, so not acting like a proper Daddy, and I can't keep up. And I actually thought she'd done a pretty good job with the spanking scene, so that's pissing me off a little.

I thought my face was burning before, but he's thrown napalm on it. And apparently some of it got into my panties, because things are on fire down there. I finally manage to spit out, "That's gross."

"You're reading that tripe and you're talking to me about gross?"

Tripe? Who the hell actually says that anymore? I almost ask him that, but his nearness, the smell of his cologne, the throbbing between my legs, all conspire to tie my tongue.

And that gives him enough time to make his move.

One hand brings the offending trade paperback down on my butt with a surprisingly firm thud. The other grabs my ponytail, uses it to propel me forward.

He forces my mouth against his. I keep my lips firmly shut.

He keeps smacking me with the book as he kisses me.

I fight it for as long as I can—fight the seductive stinging against my ass, fight the mixture of arousal and alarm flooding me. Finally, my lips open, and I melt against him and let him plunder my mouth. He's hard against my bare thigh, and that's killing me. I want to rub myself against it, but that's just not what a girl does to her Daddy.

"I think," Daddy says, "that you need to be punished—to know what a proper spanking feels like so you'll know when you're reading bad porn. Don't you agree, Cherise?"

I pretend to consider the question. My face is scarlet, I can tell, and my white cotton hipster panties are soaked through, and even though things have gotten weird, I know what answer is expected of me. "I've been a bad girl, Daddy. I deserve to be punished."

I look contrite and nervous. He looks stern and annoyed, but eager at the same time.

Then we both start laughing—first him, then me, laughing and holding each other, his hard body pressed against me. His lips press against my hair, and he whispers, still chuckling, "I love you."

We both rearrange our faces appropriately, he to the stern father, I to the nervous teenager. I wonder if it's as hard for him as it is for me.

He sits on the sofa, pulls me roughly over his knee. "Daddy, please..." I protest. It sounds more like I'm begging for him to give me the spanking I crave.

Which is true. Very little here is what it seems.

"Daddy" is my lover, Mike, not my father. My name isn't Cherise, either; it's Kaitlyn. The fake name helps me separate. Otherwise I don't think I could let myself indulge in these punishment fantasies, let alone the semi-incestuous ones. It's a trick I learned from the ex-boyfriend who lured me into his kinky world of spanking and erotic role-play, and one I've taught Mike.

I'd never let myself be spanked before I learned that trick. I had too much trouble letting go of my real-life doctor self, and all its responsibilities, to indulge my spanking-and-discipline fantasies. Making it all a game, with the spanker and spankee both characters, allows me to have my fun without giving up any real power or control. Besides, I like the whole package:

the role-play, the costumes, the way it lets us toy with taboos without actually violating them.

Only today it's all going a bit oddly.

At this point I should be deep into role-playing teenage Cherise, scared because she's in trouble and because her Daddy's crossing lines that fathers shouldn't cross. To make it worse for her, Cherise thinks her Dad's a Hot Older Man, the kind she'd have fantasies about if he was someone else's father, and wrong as it is, she's getting turned on. It's a game we've played often before, and it always works.

But right now I'm thrown. Excited, but thrown. Mike's deviated from the script. He was supposed to "find" and react to the cigarettes, not the novel.

Bringing the book into it is getting too close to reality for my taste. I don't want to feel like Mike's spanking me for something that bugs him in real life—and while it doesn't make sense that he'd suddenly be offended by my taste in novels, I'm not sure why else he'd bring the book into it.

Of course, my brain's not working at one hundred percent right now because the blood that's supposed to power it has rushed to my clit. I'm easy to confuse in this state.

We're not following the script anymore, the script that keeps my fantasies safe. But even though my head's in a bit of an uproar, I'm still wet and still eager to have Mike—Daddy, I mean—paddle my ass.

He flips up my short plaid skirt. Runs his hand over my cotton-clad ass. I force myself to squirm away, but I'm sure he can tell I'm rubbing myself against him, not trying to escape.

"You've been bad, Cherise. I'm going to spank your bare bottom, like the heroine in that appalling book." It sounds so corny that I can't help laughing, although I try to disguise it with a groan.

I want to remind him he groans over some of the writing in some of his thrillers and still gets sucked into the story—but I'm afraid if I do, I'll blow the mood, blow being Cherise, miss out on my spanking.

He hooks his fingers in the elastic waistband of my panties. As Cherise, I should be struggling and protesting, but instead I raise my hips and wiggle to make it easier for him to yank them down. Sometimes it's hard to make myself fight back when I want it this badly.

Then I spread my legs so he can see how wet I am.

I know Mike wants to touch, but he's not Mike now, he's Daddy, and Daddy just chuckles deep in his throat. "Poor little girl. That's what happens when you read too much smut."

He plants one hand on the back of my head to keep me in place.

The other one starts spanking.

Sometimes he starts off hard and fast, going for a sharp build to crescendo. This time, he opens soft and sensual, little teasing pats that make me want to purr, that bring the blood to my ass-cheeks gradually. I raise my butt, eager for more, and he gives me more, going faster and harder, building a rhythm.

Soon, my ass feels huge and hot and tender, but in a good way, like huge and hot and tender is its proper state, and I've been waiting for years, not knowing what I was missing, for someone to repair my sad unspanked bottom. My entire body tingles, alive and excited by the smacks on my ass, the firm, controlling hand on the back of my head. I can't get away, I don't want to get away, I want to lie forever over Mike's lap as his hand smacks down on my ass and thighs.

No. Daddy's lap. Mike doesn't spank me.

Mike's lap? Daddy's lap?

Hell, I'm not sure who I am at the moment. Cherise and

Kaitlyn blur together into a creature of pure sensation who just wants to enjoy this wonderful spanking.

Every time his hand smacks down, I rise up to meet it. Every time he lifts his hand again, I grind my bare mound as best I can against his corduroy-covered thigh. It's a slow build, each slap and each grind getting me closer to orgasm without pushing me over the edge.

Close. So close.

The room's gone. My mind is gone. There's nothing left in this world but my throbbing ass and my straining, swollen clit, and Daddy's hand, Daddy's body, the smell of Daddy surrounding me, Daddy's voice telling me what a naughty, naughty girl I am.

But when the orgasm takes me, throws me even farther from normal reality, forces a scream from my throat, what I cry out isn't "Daddy!" but "Mike!"

He pulls me up, helps me sit on his lap. Every ridge of the corduroy is an exquisite torture to my sore butt. I wrap my arms around his neck and cuddle close, feeling small and safe and very much loved.

As I start to come down from the heights, I realize I'd called him by the "wrong" name, try to recover with "I love you, Daddy."

He kisses the top of my head. "I think I liked it better when you called me Mike. Maybe we can save Cherise and Daddy for special occasions and just be you and me when I spank you."

I go from warm and fuzzy to anxious in a heartbeat, not sure I like where he's going. He notices, I think, because he kisses me so sweetly and deeply that my body turns to liquid. Then he slips his hand between my thighs and with a few flicks of his finger on my already sensitive clit, liquid becomes light and I'm flying again.

This is something that Daddy never does to Cherise. Cherise may get off on being spanked, and Daddy may say and do things that would be inappropriate for a real father, but he never does anything directly sexual. Caressing me is for Mike, not Daddy.

So is fucking me, and when he lifts me up so he can unzip his pants and take out his cock, I think that I could get used to Mike rather than Daddy doing the spanking if it ends like this.

After he pulls me down to straddle his cock, filling me like I didn't know I ached to be filled, he starts smacking my tender ass. This time there's no doubt at all who's doing the spanking because his cock is deep inside me and my eyes are locked into his and he's saying my own name. This time, when I shudder and scream, it's with Mike.

Yum. Spanking and fucking, two great tastes that taste great together, far better than peanut butter and chocolate. It's just... it's just not something I've ever let myself do before. My ex liked to keep it separate, and it was easier, safer, that way.

He feels my body tense, asks me what's wrong. I sort through a few variations before finding the right words. "That was great. But I don't want you punishing me. That's what Daddy's for— so it's not real and I can enjoy the spanking."

I didn't think he could pull me any closer, but he manages to. "Kaitlyn, sweetheart, you know this isn't punishment. It's fun. Sometimes I'd rather just be me, spanking the woman I love."

"But...the book. You were scolding me. I don't like that."

"Oh, shit, you weren't supposed to take that seriously! That was part of the game."

Then he makes a weird face. "Besides, I picked that one off the bedside table because the cover picture was sexy and...well, the next thing I knew it was three hours later."

"Ha! Told you they were addictive!"

He goes on. He loves to talk about books. "I loved the bit

you'd bookmarked because the heroine was so open about liking to be spanked—and the hero is like me, loving how much it turns her on. I wanted to read it out loud during our scene, but I couldn't figure out how to do it and still sound like Daddy."

I feel a weight sink off me and through the floor. Now that we've tried it, I'd like good clean spanky fun mixed with fucking on a more regular basis, and I think I can even admit that now.

But a bit of me is disappointed. When an ER doctor has a bad day at work, it's *really* bad. I want to make everything better, to save everyone, to get the world back under control, and I can't. When I get home after a day like that, shucking being a grown-up and being bratty Cherise taken in hand by Daddy is exactly what I need.

It isn't easy for me to say so in as many words, but after several false starts, I manage to get it out.

"That makes sense, Kaitlyn. I love spanking you because it's fun and turns you on, but I definitely see why being Cherise is good for you sometimes—and I like that you like it." He changes his voice to the stern Daddy-voice. "And young lady, if you start acting up, and especially if I catch you with cigarettes, your Daddy is going to punish you!"

And what I say to that, since I'm not Cherise at the moment, is "Yum!"

POWER
OVER POWER

Emerald

I pulled open the glass door against the glaring Saturday morning sun. The heavily windowed walls offered little relief from its brightness as I blinked and looked around the lobby.

Dominic sat at his desk across from the front counter. One month before, I had watched Dominic on the first night of class as he stood at the front of the studio and introduced the defense system in which he would be training us. The students stood in a row in front of him, dressed the same way he was in sneakers, black T-shirts with the royal blue KRAV MAGA logo on the chest, and loose, lightweight black pants with matching royal blue stripes down the sides.

"Krav Maga is not like traditional martial arts," he had explained. "Traditional martial arts involve sparring, a back-and-forth, a focus on skill. Krav Maga is about dropping somebody—knocking someone out within ten seconds so you can get away." He met the eyes of each student in the line in front of him. "It's also not about size. The point of Krav is that it puts everyone on an equal playing field, focusing on universal vulnerabilities that anyone can exploit, regardless of size."

His voice was calm, assured, serious. I had watched him, captivated. Dominic didn't necessarily look like a self-defense expert. He was only slightly taller than I was, probably five foot ten. His build was slim and athletic. The denseness of his muscles, however, was evident not only under the short sleeves of his T-shirt but also in the resounding thuds that reverberated off the studio walls as he demonstrated kicks and punches, and used knees and elbows on the punching bag at the front of the room as the students watched in silence.

Despite the subject matter, there was no bravado or machismo in his countenance. I had seen from the pictures and accompanying labels hanging in the lobby that Dominic instructed in traditional martial arts as well as Krav Maga. While I had never taken any myself, I sensed in him the understated confidence I had observed before in martial artists—an exquisite self-possession and understanding of their capabilities, the assurance that there was no need to prove anything to anyone. It was like they had power over their own power. It served them rather than the other way around. There was no compulsion to use it, to put it on display; it was just there, second nature, if it was ever needed.

Dominic looked up at my entrance.

"Hi, Jackie."

I smiled at him and glanced at the clock. Saturday morning class was optional, a makeup class for those who missed any of the three sessions held during the week or who just wanted an extra review. I was only about five minutes early, but there didn't seem to be anyone else around.

He followed my gaze. "You're the only one here so far. People often trickle in around starting time on Saturdays. You can have a seat if you want, or go on in and start warming up."

I sat on the bench perpendicular to his desk, and he smiled and turned back to his computer. I didn't need to look at Dominic to feel the way he was affecting me. It happened just from being in the same room with him. It was something that went beyond looks, beyond personality, beyond simple attraction. It was pure heat, like a raw power of undiluted wanting, craving, hunger. I felt it when I watched the nonchalance with which he taught the methodology used by the Israeli army for hand-to-hand combat, a methodology designed, ultimately, to kill people. I watched the skill, control, and focus of the lightning flashes of movement, the cracking thuds that seemed effortless to him, and felt the raw heat in my core. Every movement he executed was exactly what was called for, nothing more, nothing less. He didn't execute power just for the sake of executing power. Power was cultivated in him so deeply that it simply came out when needed.

I wanted to fuck him so badly I could hardly stand still.

Five minutes later he glanced at the clock again. "Hmm. Maybe people had a little too much partying on a Friday night," he chuckled as he stood up. "I've never had attendance this low on a Saturday."

"Yeah, I imagine you want to cancel," I babbled, standing nervously.

Dominic shrugged. "It's up to you. You can certainly take off if you'd like. If you want to stay, I'll work you."

A shiver went through me, and I tried not to shudder visibly. I glanced around, not sure if I *did* want to take the class with Dominic all by myself. I knew his focus was strictly professional, and I might end up making a fool of myself as I practically drooled over him.

"Uh, okay. If you don't mind," I responded, my mouth appearing to ignore all the considerations that had just run through my mind.

"No, come on in," he said, indicating the studio with a jerk of his head and leading me into it. I moved to the far end toward the supply room and set my bag and purse down on the bench.

As we began stretching, my breath quickened. The training hadn't even begun, and already I knew this was a mistake. I wasn't going to be able to handle this kind of undivided attention from Dominic. Even if he were interested in what I was, which I had no reason to believe he was, the studio's walls were made of glass, making the view from the street wide open. He wasn't about to fuck me with that kind of visibility.

I had to get out of there.

"Okay, you remember the way we learned early in the week to defend against a choke hold?" Dominic asked.

"Yeah," I answered, clearing my throat. Dominic approached me, and I almost backed up, not trusting myself if he touched me.

"Show me what you remember." He reached forward and placed both hands around my neck, facing me. My breath caught, and I snapped my hands up and slammed my forearms into his, breaking the grip.

"Good," he said, stepping back. "Let's try it up against the wall."

I was painfully aware of my ragged breathing and the wetness between my legs as Dominic leaned into me, wrapping his hands around my neck and pushing me back against the wall. I defended again and had to consciously resist pressing my hand between my legs.

"Okay, grab a kick shield," Dominic said, nodding at a stack in the corner of the room. "I'm going to demonstrate the kick we learned on Wednesday. Remember, start with your weight on the kicking foot—hop quickly to the other foot and kick while you're in the air. The momentum increases your power. Then recoil immediately. Always recoil right away. Limbs not up against you are vulnerable to being grabbed."

I nodded, trying to focus. Dominic backed up, and I crouched in position with the kick pad in front of me. Dominic's foot snapped forward, and I was almost knocked backward by the force of the impact even as the padding absorbed most of it. I shuddered as I imagined what such a blow would be like without the shield.

"Your turn," Dominic took the pad from me.

I did my best to kick the sexual frustration out of me as I slammed first my right then my left foot into the kick pad with a grunt. I alternated back and forth until Dominic told me to stop.

The elevated heart rate and adrenaline pumping through me had not served the desired purpose at all.

"Do you remember the series we learned earlier in the week?" Dominic demonstrated in the air the series of punches, kicks, and elbow slams to get out of a headlock and render the assailant to the ground. I nodded.

"Okay, let's try it." Dominic fitted his arm around my neck from behind and held firmly. My breath caught, and I almost pressed back against him. I caught myself and mimed the series, stopping each move just short of actual impact with him. My breath was ragged when I finished. The tingling in my pussy had reached the point of distraction.

"Are you okay?" Dominic asked.

"Yeah," I squeaked out, almost wincing at the hoarseness of my voice. I cleared my throat. "Fine. Go right ahead," I said, managing to make my voice sound almost normal.

He turned me around and grabbed me around the neck again, and immediately I couldn't breathe—and it wasn't because his hold was too strong. I started the series, slamming my elbow back toward his chest, halting right before it made contact with him. Suddenly I forgot the next move and stopped.

"Don't stop," Dominic said. "Don't ever stop, Jackie."

"I forgot the next move," I stared to explain as Dominic turned me around.

"I know you did. But you're training yourself all the time here, and you don't ever want to train yourself to pause or freeze. If you forget what you're doing"—his eyes were serious as they penetrated mine—"just start throwing punches."

I held his gaze and managed to nod.

He backed up. "You want to grab some water?"

I nodded again and walked over to my bag as he moved to the side of the room to put the kick shield back. I took a drink, facing the bench, and set my water bottle down.

Suddenly a body was up against me from behind, arm rough around my neck. I was in a headlock. It took me just a second to realize I needed to defend myself, and I snapped an elbow back and tried to whirl, realizing it was too late.

Dominic whipped me around and pressed me against the wall. "Okay, you weren't expecting me there. You weren't ready, and you paused. *Assailants don't wait until you're ready.* You have to be prepared all the time." He eased his hold on me and backed up. I was breathless, staring in his eyes as my pussy tingled insistently.

"I'm going to grab some gloves," he said, moving to the supply room a few feet away.

He opened the door and disappeared through it as I stared at it. I swallowed. As if drawn by a magnet, my feet began to step toward the supply room. The door was open, and I could hear Dominic rummaging around inside as I approached. I reached the door and silently stepped through it.

Dominic had his back to me. He pulled a pair of gloves from the top of a pile and turned, stopping when he saw me.

I was already in the room, where I wasn't supposed to be. There was no way to back out gracefully now. For a few seconds there was silence.

"I want you to—" my voice, already tiny and faltering, failed me after those four words.

Dominic took a step forward, his expression questioning. He raised his eyebrows and cocked an ear toward me. "You want what?"

My breathing was uneven; I felt like I did when I was already close to orgasm. The intensity wasn't lending itself to articulation. I moved forward as well.

"I want," my voice halted again, but this time only for a split second. "I want you to fuck me."

I whispered it, knowing I was barely audible, and looked down at the ground, my cheeks flaming. I felt Dominic's eyes on me and told myself the worst he could do was say no, and I could turn around and leave and never come back. The all-encompassing fixation of wanting him overruled humiliation in me as the room stayed silent for a few seconds.

Dominic's motions were deliberate as he moved toward and then past me. My eyes widened. I didn't move.

The door closed. The quiet, solid thud as I sensed that he was still in the room with me sent a jolt of heat through me that almost made me dizzy. I barely breathed as I started to turn around.

But he was already back in front of me. He moved in so that he was almost touching me, close enough that I felt weak, but not actually making contact. He looked down at me.

"You want me to fuck you," he repeated. His tone was neutral.

I trembled, wanting to touch him but feeling frozen. Still

looking at the ground, I nodded.

With characteristic efficiency of motion, he reached with one finger and pulled my chin up. A shudder ran through me as I felt his power—the power I saw in every move he made, that he exuded at the front of the class, that he spoke when he told us what we were capable of, that coiled and expelled from him whenever he slammed any part of his body into the punching bag. This was the power that lived unquestioned within him, so seamlessly that it was as though it wouldn't exist without him.

I moved my eyes to his. Dominic pushed forward and kissed me, hard, his body pressing against mine as I hit the wall behind me. I thrashed against him, my hands ripping at his T-shirt as I fought to breathe. I felt like I could already come.

Dominic placed a hand behind my neck and gripped my waist, pulling my body even closer to his. I pulled at his shirt again and he let go of me and stripped it off, reaching to pull mine off as well before returning his hands to the solid grip of my body and my mouth to his unrelenting kiss. I could feel his erection against me as he slowed down and eased back.

"We'd need a condom," he whispered, looking down at me.

My eyes felt out of focus as I looked back at him. "I have some in my purse," I whispered back, barely recognizing my own voice.

Dominic stepped back, and I walked shakily to the door in my pants, sneakers, and sports bra. I opened it and stepped through, blinking at the sunlight streaming in through the glass walls. It felt like a different world.

I retrieved my purse and reentered the supply room unsteadily. As I stepped through the door, Dominic's hard chest hit me from behind, his arm instantaneously around my neck. I drew a quick breath and rammed my elbow to within an inch of his chest, my own chest heaving.

He whirled me around and pushed me back up against the wall.

"Good reaction time that time," he said, his voice low. "Particularly under the circumstances." I felt the hardness of his cock pressing against my hip. Slowly, he brought one hand up to grip my throat, then the other to join it.

"You know what to do now?" His voice was a whisper. The question wasn't really a question. We had just practiced it in the studio.

I nodded. He looked at me, not moving.

"I don't want to," I whispered. I heard the tremble in my voice.

Dominic nodded slowly, eyes still on mine. He could have held me in place with them alone. He moved one hand to stroke a finger along my jawline, his eyes following it. His other hand stayed in place at my throat. He licked his lips and looked back at me.

Suddenly his grip tightened as he lifted me up against the wall by my neck. My jaw dropped, feet hanging loosely without the ground beneath them. I was exactly at eye level with Dominic now, his hand against the sides of my neck in a way that somehow barely hurt.

My pussy started to drip.

Dominic's eyes blazed into mine as he reached and ran a finger from my collarbone down to the top of my sports bra. Slowly he lowered me back to the ground and pushed my sports bra up, grabbing my breasts with a firmness just short of painful. My breath came to a fiery halt in my throat.

"Breathe," he whispered, looking into my eyes. It was an order he often gave during class. I obeyed, expelling the breath caught in my throat and deliberately guiding in another one.

Dominic reached up and removed my ponytail holder, then

yanked my bra over my head and pulled me forward. He guided me across the room to a stack of floor mats about waist high. Pressing me up against them, he ran his hand up the back of my neck and grabbed my hair near my scalp. I whimpered as he kissed me, involuntarily gyrating against him. He lowered his hands and yanked my pants and panties down to my knees, lifting me to the stack of mats and pulling them the rest of the way off almost before I realized what was happening. I kicked my sneakers off and looked at him, breathing heavily.

Dominic lifted me back to the ground and turned me around, one hand holding my hip, the other tracing lightly over the front of my body. His fingers strayed casually, rising over the swell of my breast, dragging lightly across the nipple, then down the other side and on to the next one. The reminder to breathe was gone. I felt like I had forgotten how.

I wanted him to throw me down, ram his cock into me and fuck me hard, take full control of me, of him, of—everything. I tried to wiggle impatiently and realized that despite the calmness of his movements, the grip he had on me was like a clothespin on tissue paper. I felt his breath on my ear, steady in comparison to my almost frantic panting. Slowly he moved his hand from my breasts to the back of my neck again, sliding up through my hair and gripping into a fist. I caught my breath.

"Well, conveniently enough, I want to fuck you, too, Jackie," he whispered smoothly, and my legs trembled. "And I think I know what you want me to do. You want me to hold you down, fuck you hard, get pretty rough with you." I wondered if, for the first time, I would come without actually being touched. "You're looking for power. In your own way, getting fucked rough like that will make you feel powerful. Is that right?" My vision was becoming fuzzy, and I could hardly make sense of the words he was saying.

Dominic let go of my hip and slid his hand across my stomach, up over my breasts and finally to my throat.

"Everything you're looking for, Jackie, you already have inside you." The tone of his whisper had changed, and I barely had time to process the words before he whipped me around, forcing my mouth open with his as he kissed me again. He held my hair in a fist of steel and moved his other hand back to my body, lightly brushing my rib cage. He pulled away and I watched the slow movement of his fingers, gliding like honey running over my skin.

I whimpered desperately. He hadn't even touched my pussy, and I felt close to a kind of climax of which I didn't know the meaning. It felt like a near euphoria combined with a vague but deep fear that together seemed to be pushing tears seriously toward the surface.

"Dominic," I pleaded. My voice trembled like a blade of grass in the breeze. He looked up at me.

I realized then what he was doing. He was making me wait, making me feel, making me experience every single nuance, every detail, everything that was in me, in my body, rather than slamming it all away.

And suddenly I wondered if that was what having power over power meant.

The tears flowed out of me like an orgasm, fully beyond my control, my breath turning to a silent sob that felt somehow calm, even peaceful, as I felt a space open up in me I wasn't sure I had ever felt before. Dominic's eyes stayed on mine.

The wave moved through me, and Dominic dropped his finger to my clit. I gasped and climaxed as soon as he moved it, orgasm bursting forth in a rush so overpowering I almost felt I would lose consciousness. Steady, unabated screams pulsed through me as Dominic held my gaze as well as my balance with his unyielding grip at my neck. When it was done I fell limp, my entire body slick with sweat, legs shaking and hanging like string over the stack of mats.

Dominic lowered me onto my back and let go of my hair, then backed up and retrieved my purse. Hands shaking, I reached and fumbled through it in my horizontal position until I found the little zippered pouch. Extracting a condom from it, I pushed it into his hand.

I heard the package rip open and my purse drop to the floor as Dominic backed up. He slid me up farther on the stack of mats and leapt lightly onto them, pushing between my legs. My eyes were closed, and I opened them as he hovered above me. I was far beyond words, knowing only what was in my body.

"Breathe," Dominic whispered again as he dropped his body onto mine, plunging into me and grasping my shoulders as his breath rushed against my ear. He thrust into me with rhythmic strength as I lay like a doll, sprawled powerlessly across the hard foam beneath me. Dominic pumped hard, holding my hips solidly. His breathing changed as he thrust just a bit harder and came inside me, my body like a deflated balloon, a beautiful, motionless receptacle for his come.

I closed my eyes again as he finished, feeling a sorrow at the impending loss of contact with his body. When he pulled out, I opened my eyes and turned to him. He leapt off the stack of mats and reached to help me down. I stopped at the edge, not ready to stand up yet.

In a daze, I looked at the floor, my body shaking. Dominic's low voice broke the silence.

"Whatever is in you, whatever you're feeling—feel it. Don't hide from it. Don't try to 'beat' it. Be with it until you understand it, until you know where it comes from." I frowned at the floor. "Then it won't rule you anymore."

I raised my eyes to his as he finished the sentence. Sweat dripped from my forehead onto my neck as my quick breaths punctuated the silence in the room.

"That's what power is," Dominic said. "It doesn't have anything to do with force or subjugation."

I looked down at his hand as he held it out to me again and allowed my body to slide off the mats. My feet on the floor felt foreign.

I gathered my clothes and dressed slowly. Dominic handed me my purse as I straightened, and we walked to the door together. I turned to him; without a word, he grabbed the back of my neck and kissed me, rendering me immediately breathless as I braced myself against the door with one hand.

He let go of me slowly. My hand slipped from the door as he took a step back.

"See you Monday." Dominic's hand brushed the small of my back once before he stepped forward and turned the knob.

THE CHAIR

Lolita Lopez

The chair was a thing of sumptuous decadence: Sleek lines. Gleaming onyx wood. That ever-so-plush leather. From the first moment she'd spied the chair, Lily had desperately wanted to sink down into its sensual embrace. It had called to her, whispering naughtily in her ear and promising a sexual experience to top all others. Even now, all these weeks later, just staring at the chair sent jittery waves through her belly.

Her vivid imagination shot into overdrive. She could almost feel the cool kiss of leather against her naked skin and the tight clinch of the padded cuffs around her ankles and wrists. The thought of being bound to the chair, helpless and completely at Cal's mercy, made her pussy pulse with need. Sticky wetness seeped between her bare thighs from sheer anticipation.

"Sit."

Cal's instruction sent white-hot shock waves through her core. Lily's nipples stood at attention. She inhaled a shuddery breath and took a tentative step forward. Skimming her fingertips over the smooth wooden arm, Lily appreciated the beauty and craftsmanship of the chair. Only a hedonist like Cal would think to commission such a hybrid piece of furniture. Part bondage device and part sex toy, it was legendary among his rather kinky circle of friends.

Before Cal, Lily had only dabbled in the lightest of kink: A silk scarf binding her wrists to a headboard. An ice cube between her lover's lips gliding over the swell of her breast. A few stinging smacks on her bottom in the heat of passion.

But then Cal had appeared in her life and introduced her to the sometimes painful but always exhilarating world of BDSM. That first night he'd broached the subject, Cal had taken her to his playroom and talked her through the various toys and implements. When he'd shown her the chair sitting in the corner on a raised platform, Lily's curiosity had been piqued. What was hidden beneath the panels spanning the distance between the chair's legs? And why did the platform require a power source? In that instant, she'd decided to accept the experience Cal offered and earn the privilege to sit on his prized piece.

"Lily."

Cal's prompt brought her back to the present. Fingers trembling with trepidation, she stepped onto the dais. Lily turned to face her lover and slowly sank down onto the wide seat. Her bare feet dangled above the platform. Her belly quivered with apprehension. She suddenly felt so young and inexperienced. Perhaps that was part of the design. Cal seemed to enjoy throwing her composure off kilter before every scene. There was something about embracing the unknown and giving her complete trust to him that amplified the experience and eventual release.

Perched on the chair, Lily eyed Cal as he moved out of the shadows. Tonight he remained fully dressed, a stark contrast to her vulnerable state and a clear reminder of his absolute control of the situation. He pocketed his platinum cufflinks and slowly rolled up the sleeves of his crisp shirt. Lily licked her lips and pressed her knees tightly together. She gripped the arms of the chair as Cal moved closer. Their gazes clashed as he wrapped the leather cuffs over her wrists. He didn't break their mutual stare as he picked up the remote control and adjusted the tilt of the chair's reclining back, pushing her hips up slightly.

He set aside the remote and knelt in front of the chair. Cal's warm breath tickled her shins as he grazed his lips over her skin and placed kisses along the curves of her knees. He buckled her ankles to the legs of the chair, forcing her thighs wide open and baring the smoothly waxed lips of her cunt to his appreciative gaze. She recognized the fiery gleam in his eyes. He'd seen the evidence of her arousal, the shiny juices seeping from her and coating her skin.

Cal brushed his knuckles over her sex. "You always get so wet."

"Only for you."

Her breathless words brought a smile to his face. Cal leaned forward and nuzzled his nose in her dripping pussy. His pointed tongue swiped her slit, flicking the stiff nub aching so desperately for his touch. Lily tried to arch her hips to meet his prodding tongue but the bonds held her in place. She whimpered in protest but Cal simply wiped his mouth with the back of his hand and backed away from her.

Lily's eyes widened as Cal removed the cloth covering the small table standing just to his left and revealed a variety of floggers, clamps and straps. She swallowed hard. He was going to drag this out and make her earn every mind-blowing orgasm.

Air hissed through her teeth at the first heavy thud of suede ribbons against her breasts. Cal wielded the flogger with the efficiency of a true master, his strikes caressing her naked skin.

She arched into the flicks, loving the sensations the gentle warm-up swats evoked. Tendrils of arousal blossomed in the pit of her belly. Heat spread across her chest and down her softly sloped stomach.

Soon Cal switched to a stiffer flogger. Lily cried out at the first stinging swat of the rigid leather tongues against her sensitized skin. The leather grazed her pebbled nipples and licked down the curved plane of her tummy. She sucked in her breath and tried to pull back to avoid the incessant flicks but it was no use. The chair's tilted back made it impossible for her to escape Cal's flogging.

Prickly heat erupted wherever the leather ribbons touched. Cal increased the tempo of his swats and allowed the stinging fingers to fall a little harder each time. When she felt the flogger's kiss moving lower, Lily shivered. She yelped at the first slap of leather against her bare pussy. With her ankles pinned and thighs spread wide, Cal had total access to the dewy center of her sex and apparently had no intention to spare her most tender place.

Her first instinct was to shout out their safeword but she shoved away the urge, determined to conquer this new and frightening sensation. She panted and tensed before every smack of the flogger. Her hips shifted from side to side in a desperate attempt to escape Cal's next swat.

And then she felt it.

Behind every stinging kiss there was the most delicious ripple vibrating her clit. Lily concentrated on that wonderfully electrifying sensation. In no time at all, she'd lifted her hips to meet every downward fall of the flogger's leather tongues. This was the place she'd learned to accept as a submissive. The sweet agony of pleasure and pain threw her senses into overdrive. Every nerve in her body flared as she hovered on the brink of explosion.

When Cal stopped unexpectedly, Lily groaned with displeasure and immediately knew she'd broken one of their established rules. During these games they played, her position was simply to accept and never to dictate. Cal clicked his teeth and shook his head. Breathing hard and trying desperately to ignore the uncomfortable pulse of her pussy, Lily warily watched her lover to see what punishment he would choose.

As if sensing her stare, Cal selected a length of black silk and applied a blindfold. Her eyesight lost, Lily waited with bated breath, her body humming nervously. Cal's fingers drifted over her breasts. In the next second, she experienced that all too familiar bite of a clothespin. A series of the wooden torture devices followed along the plump swell of her breasts.

As she acclimated to the pinching sensation, Lily felt her bottom drop a bit. With a push of a button, Cal had removed a center strip of the seat. It noiselessly slid down into the base and presented Cal with complete access to her naughty bits. Exposed to his mercy, Lily could only wonder what might come next. Her clit was still swollen and just a few flicks away from sending her into a screaming orgasm.

She stilled as Cal drew closer, his body heat penetrating her skin. His warm breath buffeted her neck. His sandalwood scent filled her nose. She moaned hungrily as his slippery fingers glided between the lips of her cunt and slid even lower to the pucker hidden there. She surrendered to his probing, allowing his fingers to relax her ass for his inevitable intrusion. Before Cal, Lily had refused to even consider that particular sex act. It was wrong and dirty.

Cal had shown her she'd been absolutely right. Anal sex was dirty—deliciously and naughtily so. And now she couldn't get enough.

His fingers disappeared. A moment later, the blunt tip of a dildo prodded her ass. So that's what was hidden beneath the seat of the chair! Cal had mounted sex toys in the compartment there. She could hear the whir of a motor as the dildo rose and fell.

Lily yielded to the pressure of the nudging dildo. It slipped inside and stretched her ring with each shallow thrust. Cal's lips were on her neck, setting her skin alight with goose bumps as the motorized dildo fucked her ass. His mouth drifted lower, skimming between her breasts and peppering a line of kisses down to her navel. His tongue circled her belly button before zigzagging right down to her dripping cunt. Hands on her inner thighs, he traced her folds with his tongue.

She was on fire. The dueling sensations of being taken by the dildo and licked by Cal threatened to send her over the edge. She tugged on her wrist cuffs, fingers itching to rake through Cal's hair, to hold his head there, just there, as she came against his mouth. She was close; so very, very close.

Cal's tongue disappeared abruptly. Lily cried out and pumped her hips as the dildo penetrated her bottom again and again. He'd stolen her orgasm and she hated him for it. At the same time, she wanted to beg him to return, to flick his tongue against her clit just one more time. But he'd only laugh at her and find a new way to tease. Her predicament was simultaneously infuriating and thrilling.

Shaking with need, Lily blinked wildly as the blindfold was whipped free. She focused on Cal's face, his stony expression betraying none of the amusement and pleasure she knew he must have been experiencing at her expense. His touch was surprisingly gentle as he caressed her cheek and pressed a kiss to her mouth. He nipped at her lower lip. "Do you want to come?"

"Yes." Her strangled reply filled the room. "Please."

The corner of his mouth lifted. "Soon."

And then he was backing away from her and picking up

his remote control again. The dildo buried deep inside her ass paused and a new silicone phallus prodded her pussy. She wiggled until it slid into place. Double penetration was fairly new to Lily. Cal had been training her over the last few weeks to accept both his cock and a dildo. Now she understood why.

With alternating thrusts, the dildos drove into her repeatedly. When Cal added another toy to the mix, an intimidating black wand with a tennis-ball-sized vibrator mounted on top, Lily went wild. There was no controlling her reaction. The buzzing ball pressed against her clit sent vibrating waves through her belly and down into her thighs. Her body tensed, toes curling, fingers clenching as she climaxed so hard she feared blacking out.

"That's it, love. Come for me."

She couldn't deny him, not now, not ever. Undulating against her bonds, Lily rode out the shocking waves of her orgasm. Every thrust of the cocks amplified the experience until it was too much. She begged Cal to stop, to take away the vibrator, but even as she pleaded for mercy, she couldn't bring herself to utter their safeword. The primitive, sex-crazed whore lurking deep inside her, the very essence of her id, had been set free. Lily was helpless to stop it now. This was going just as far as Cal cared to take it.

Just as Lily surged into another orgasm, Cal picked up a flogger and expertly flicked the leather ribbons against the clothespins clinging to her breasts. They snapped free and clattered to the ground. Lily shrieked as intensely sharp pain mixed with the unbelievable ecstasy of her forced climax exploded in her core. The flogger slapped against her flushed skin again and again. Her mind reeled as she swung from one extreme to the other. Pain. Pleasure.

Lily's orgasms changed from separate events to one long and

unending oscillation of bliss. She barely registered the disappearance of the vibrator and dildo that had been stimulating her pussy. The rubber cock remained in her ass, its speed kicked up a few notches. Cal's fingers replaced the other dildo. He hovered over her, his knee wedged against hers on the lip of the chair, and finger-fucked her cunt until she thought she just might die.

"You know what I want." His fingers bumped her G-spot relentlessly. His thumb massaged tight circles around her inflamed clit.

She shook her head. Embarrassment stained her cheeks even as she hovered on the brink of coming again. "I can't."

"You can." His calm tone pierced the fever pitch. "And you will."

And she did. Like before, she found it impossible to deny Cal. She surrendered completely to the almost irritating urge his thrusting fingers evoked. Screaming like a banshee, Lily squirted all over his hand, her juices running along his wrist and forearm. Cal growled with appreciation as she skyrocketed to a new place, a place of such intense ecstasy she couldn't think, could hardly breathe. She was simply a vessel for the most rapturous sensations imaginable.

At some point, Lily blacked out, her mind simply unable to process the overwhelming explosion of orgasmic wonder. When she came to, her wrists and ankles had been freed from their bonds. Cal knelt between her thighs and lapped languidly at her, his talented tongue gathering her slick cream and teasing her into awareness.

With a heavy sigh, Lily reached down and ran her fingers through his fine hair. In the gentle moments like this, Cal showed her just how much he truly loved her. The contrast between this Cal and the man who sometimes subjected her to painful sensual tortures was as different as night and day—just as the girl who allowed Cal to dominate her was nothing like the no-nonsense, ball-breaking Lily who lectured on feminism to a hall of half-asleep undergrads three days a week. Theirs was a complex relationship and one she wouldn't have traded for anything in the world.

"So," Cal said, his lips brushing her inner thigh, "what do we think of my little contraption?"

Lily gave a purr of satisfaction. With an impish smile curving her mouth, she bent down and captured his lips. "I think we should have one built for you."

Cal's eyes lit up at her suggestion. He grinned and nipped at her belly. "You'd have to shine a hell of a lot of boots before you'd earn enough points to take the reins over me."

"What can I say?" She shrugged and gave him a saucy wink. "I'm turning out to be quite the glutton for punishment."

WITHOUT EYES

Terri Pray

Susan paced across the bedroom, her heart racing. He was late. He was never late, so what was going on? He always called if something went wrong and he'd been delayed, so where was he? She glanced at the clock for the tenth time in the past twenty minutes. This just wasn't like him. Had he been in an accident?

The sound of the car pulling into the driveway silenced her fears, for now at least, and turned them into something else. Anger. If he was all right, why hadn't he called to let her know he'd be late?

"Susan?" he called out, the door slamming shut behind him. "Where are you?"

"Up here." *Up here steaming and about ready to explode!* No, she couldn't tell him that. Keep calm, keep focused, and don't let him see just how angry she was. There'd be a perfectly good explanation as to why he was late. She had to believe that.

Tom smiled as he walked into the bedroom, holding a black

and green plastic bag. "I brought something home for us."

Shopping? He'd been shopping? "Where the hell have you been, I've been worried sick!"

He blinked and took a step back. "Where did that come from?"

"You're late. You always call if you're going to be late. In five years you've never missed calling me. I've been worried out of my mind."

He flushed, then paled, looking away, the bag shifting from one hand to the other. "I'm sorry, I just got distracted. I had this idea and well…"

"You didn't think!" Her hands itched. She'd never felt more tempted to smack him in her entire life. "You were thoughtless and didn't stop to think how I'd feel!"

"Hey, I said I was sorry."

"Do you think that makes me feel any better?"

His gaze narrowed as he tossed the bag onto the bed. "I had something planned for us both, but right now it looks like you need a lesson in respect. Or have you forgotten just who is in charge of this household?"

Her heart skipped a beat and she lowered her hands to her sides. "I'm sorry, I wasn't thinking straight, sir."

"I should put you over my knee, but I have a better idea. One that will remind you of your place, my girl." He tapped one hand against his thigh. "Go and shower, settle your mind, and return to me."

Susan let out a long, slow breath. She'd gotten off lightly and she knew it, but still, she'd had a reason to be angry with him and maybe he'd taken that into account. "Yes, sir, and I'm sorry. I was just worried and then angry. I'll try to do better."

"Yes, you will." The warning was all too clear in his voice.

She cursed herself as she turned and walked out of the bedroom into the bathroom, turning the shower on and closing the door. This was one of the few places where she was permitted a little privacy. Now she wasn't sure if she'd be allowed to keep the door closed after the way she'd spoken to him.

A long shower. Maybe that would help? It couldn't hurt. At least this way she could relax and forget her tension.

Steam curled upward, seeping over the top of the shower curtain, and she dropped her clothing into the basket before stepping into the warm water. She closed her eyes before turning her head into the water, enjoying the heated massage of wet fingers that played across her face.

Less than five minutes later she stepped out of the shower and wrapped a thick, warm towel about her body. It had helped. The hot water had washed away some of her tension, and she now felt ready to face him. She only hoped he wasn't still angry with her—not that she wouldn't have deserved it if he was.

With the towel dropped into the laundry hamper she walked out of the bathroom and into the bedroom and knelt at the foot of the bed, her thighs spread, hands lightly placed on her still damp legs, her gaze lowered. A soft tremble washed through her body, her nerves threatening to get the better of her. She'd lost her temper, something she'd struggled with for years. Even though she'd had good reason, she knew better. She knew how to handle it. Ask instead of demand. Ranting and raving only meant she'd failed.

"I was angry with you, when you snapped at me, but I know that it was partially my fault. I do normally call and you were worried because I don't, normally, change my habits. However, the fact that you snapped does show that you need a reminder of just who is in charge in this house." His voice was calm as he spoke, standing naked in their room. The play box stood open at the side of the bed.

"Yes, sir. I'm sorry, I should have found a way to control my temper."

"Stand."

Susan moved to her feet quickly.

"Hands behind your back."

She swallowed hard and crossed her wrists in the small of her back.

"Don't move until I tell you otherwise." He bent over, picking up two items from the play box before he walked behind her. Soft cuffs were locked on her wrists, holding them in place. She trembled even as he checked the cuffs, knowing that she would be forbidden the use of her hands for whatever he had in mind.

Then he bound the blindfold about her eyes, stealing her sight.

"You will serve me, like this, and perhaps remember some of our early days together when you strove to find a way to please me. You've forgotten how it felt then, how you needed to do your best—this will remind you." He pulled her back a step from the bed and moved in front of her, sitting down on the edge of the bed. "Your mouth, lips, tongue, cheeks; all of these you will use to please me. Is that understood?"

"Yes, sir." Her stomach knotted.

"Then do it."

Susan lowered slowly to her knees, edging closer to him as she felt him part his thighs so she could ease between them. Her breasts brushed against his inner thighs as she settled herself into position. Her nipples crinkled into hardened points, her breath catching in the back of her throat. His presence filled her senses, his aroma tempting her closer. Without her sight, everything else became sharper.

"That's it, find your way. You know how to please me. Use that knowledge now."

Normally she used her hands. This time she couldn't; she couldn't stroke his inner thighs like she was used to.

But she could kiss them.

She twisted, lowering her head a little more, suddenly aware of how her hair brushed his thighs and the way he quivered at the touch. Susan pressed her lips against his inner thigh, kissing softly, feeling the play of muscles beneath his skin as she began to lick and nibble her way inward.

He groaned, the low sound urging her onward.

She took her time: Tasting him. Licking. Tracing the tip of her tongue over his skin in long, slow, swirls.

"Yes, that's it, my girl."

His. She'd been his for many years now and would always be his.

His cock thickened, brushing against her cheek as she worked her way slowly in. His erection throbbed, the scent of his arousal filled her nose, his heavy sac hung close, touching her chin as she turned her head to lick, softly, across the length of his cock. It took her a moment before she could find and capture the head of his cock in her lips, but she managed it, and groaned at the taste, his arousal coating the smooth skin, seeping into her mouth as she drew it in a little at a time, licking, suckling his cock.

"Yes." The word was little more than a hiss from the man she loved and had submitted to years ago.

A wicked smile claimed her lips. Slow. She'd take this slow. Tease him. Torment him. Show him everything she'd learned about him. Just because she was submissive didn't mean that, even now with her hands bound and her sight stolen, she didn't have the power. Especially now.

She flicked her tongue rapidly across the head of his cock, sucking hard until she felt a deep rocking work through his hips, then she pulled back, opening her mouth and letting his cock slide out between her lips, over her tongue.

"Hey—what are you up to?" His words were a groan, his cock pressing against her cheek as she turned her head to seek out his other thigh with her lips.

Susan didn't speak; instead she scraped her teeth carefully over the tender skin of his inner thigh. His thigh shook, his breath catching, his body tense as she nipped and licked her way back to his knee, moving away from his cock and the center of his desire.

"Wicked wench."

Yes, I am.

"You know what I want."

Yes, I do.

"Teasing me. You'll pay for it, of course."

Counting on it. She licked around his knee and knelt up, arching her back. With her hands bound behind her back, she knew the position would lift her breasts up for him, displaying her body for his view. Not enough; she could do more, she knew that. Slowly, carefully, she lifted up from her heels, tipping her hips, swaying them softly from side to side, circling them deeply as she danced on her knees for him.

His thighs tightened on either side of her body. "Susan..."

"Don't you like what you see, sir?"

"Yes, but..."

"Then let me please you. It's what you told me to do."

He couldn't argue with that one and fell silent.

Slowly, she turned her body, never moving from her knees, stretching, arching, her hips dancing, never ceasing the sensual patterns. Her skin heated, her core rippling as she moved, knowing what her dance was doing to him. The sight of her nude, bound, and blindfolded form writhing for him, only for him, aroused him. She didn't need to see him to know that.

His breathing became ragged; his thighs tensed on either side of her body. Any moment now she expected him to reach for her and drag her down until her mouth was forced back onto his cock. But she was in control here. She would show him just how well his wife knew him.

Just when she thought she had pushed too far, she stopped and lowered down once more, edging back in, nuzzling her way to his groin. Her hair brushed over his cock and balls, teasing them; she blew against his balls, taking care not to catch the head of his cock, then tickled over his heavy sac with the tip of her tongue. He groaned above her, his hips rolling, hunger clear in his body.

Now.

Susan licked softly around his sac, feeling his balls tighten within the soft skin. Then she moved slowly upward, tracing the tip of her tongue over his sac until she found the base of his cock. It throbbed beneath her gentle touch. Heat coated her inner walls. She knew, by the time she had brought him to his release, she would be aching for his touch in return.

She had to focus on him, not on her own desires right now.

Her lips closed around the tip of his cock, his taste heady as she swept her tongue over the smooth surface, dipping into his slit, tasting him deeply. His thick cock throbbed in her mouth; his hips rolled, sliding farther into her mouth as she wrapped her tongue around his needful erection.

Susan purred into his cock, feeling the vibrations play from her mouth directly onto him; the reaction was instantaneous. Tom's fingers slid into her hair, fisting, holding her tight. His hips rolled, thrusting deep into her mouth, taking her, his balls slapping against her chin.

She relaxed, her throat welcoming his cock as he claimed her mouth. *Soon, so soon.* Only now did she realize the tables had turned. She was helpless. In his grasp. She couldn't stop him: Bound. Blindfolded. Gagged with his cock, but she welcomed this, knowing she'd driven him to this point. Her touches, her knowledge, had forced him to the brink of self-control.

"God!" he cried out above her, his thrusts harder than before, his grip in her hair almost painful, but she didn't care. "Going to…"

His taste, then—thick, hot, ropey threads of his salty orgasm flooded her mouth, forcing her to swallow. Only when he shuddered and finally eased back from her lips could she take a clear breath. Silent, trembling, she knelt at the foot of the bed, his grip no longer in her hair. Her body was coated in small beads of sweat; her inner walls rippling, coated with her own need, but she knew if that was to be sated, it would be at his desire, his whim, not hers.

This was the life she had chosen. The life she had welcomed.

He brushed the back of his fingers over her cheek, his voice husky. "Well done, mine."

Susan leaned into his touch, his words wrapping around her heart in a loving cocoon. This was the life she still desired with him.

THE HARDEST PART

Alison Tyler

I'm over his lap. I've been needing a spanking for too long, and he's been making me wait. In spite of everything I've done, he's ignored the signals. I've been bratty. I've been bad. I may as well have worn a T-shirt with the words SPANK ME in bold scarlet letters across the front.

I've been that desperate.

But now that I'm here, I'd rather be anywhere else. Name the place, and I'd rather be there: in line at the DMV; waiting in the doctor's office; sitting at the back of coach on a packed flight.

I'm scared, more scared than usual, because he's taking his time. I stare at the floor, at the swirls of crimson and emerald and cornflower blue in the Oriental carpet. I stare at the ornate carved wood of the antique chair legs. I stare at his engineer boots, the scuffed black leather; boots we bought together ten years ago on Melrose, boots I've seen quite often from this position.

The air seems to shimmer in front of me.

The blood pounds in my ears.

Why was I in such a rush to find myself over his lap? What was so urgent about him paddling my ass?

I know exactly what he's doing as he strokes me through my short pleated skirt. He's taking his time to let me think of all of my transgressions. He's letting the moment sink in.

With infinite slowness, he slips my panties down my legs. My knickers are pink with hearts printed in a row, and now, they dangle from my ankles: not on, not off. I'm primed, ass up, totally exposed, waiting. He has to start now, doesn't he? He *has* to spank me now.

But he won't be rushed. Instead, he strokes my bare skin with his palm. There is no pain yet. There is only that rush of fear, starting in the base of my stomach and radiating outward.

Just spank me, I want to scream. *Please...just...spank... me...*

But he doesn't. He makes me wait.

And fuck Tom Petty for being right. The waiting *is* the hardest part. I force myself to be mute, eyes clenched shut, heart pounding so fast, so loud. If he had started right away, it'd be halfway over by now. My feet would be kicking. I'd be trying to stay still, but failing. I'd be crying, almost begging, instead of being lost here in this horrible zone, this no man's land of misery.

I arch upward, trying to tell him with my body what I need him to do. Trying to insist from a submissive position what must happen.

To my horror, he simply pets me some more, soft gentle strokes on my naked ass, until I can't help myself: I laugh. And that's when he says—oh, fuck him. *Fuck* him— "You think this is funny?"

My "No" is a whisper.

"Then why are you laughing?"

"I don't know."

"You better come up with a reason pretty damn fast."

I'm facedown, over his lap, with my idiotic heart-patterned knickers dangling from my ankles. My face is flushed. My eyes sting already with tears. And still the silent laughter shakes me. I bite my lip, hard enough to leave marks, and pray that he'll start.

"Why are you laughing?" His tone is beyond menacing. If his tone could cut, I'd be bleeding.

"I don't know," I tell him honestly—because I don't. I don't have any idea why I'm laughing. "I'm sorry," I try next.

Then he says those words, those magic words. "No, you're not. But you will be."

Finally, his hand comes down, hard. Then again, just as hard. He doesn't hesitate now. He spanks steadily, with force, driving out the worries. Driving out the fear.

With the pain comes the relief.

I won't laugh any more now.

We both know that.

I won't laugh for a long time.

RAPUNZEL

Jacqueline Applebee

My ex-girlfriend, Lola, used to tell me that a woman's hair was her beauty. Lola had warm brown skin and dreads that sprouted this way and that over her head. She told me it wasn't always this way. Lola had a grandmother in Jamaica who would straighten her hair with a vicious hot comb every Saturday night, so she'd be ready for church in the morning. Lola would recount tales of having her Afro hair painfully pressed and combed without mercy as a child, which had eliminated any trace of frizz or kinkiness. When she had rebelled against her family's control, her hair was the first thing to go wild.

My own hair was naturally straight, mousy and nothing special except that it was very long. When Lola and I had become lovers, she always liked to pull on my hair, clutching it, yanking me about and generally using it to control me in a delightful way.

Lola had introduced me to her craftsman friend, Ash, months ago, and we'd been good pals ever since. He was the one who had suggested I do something special with my natural qualities. He wanted to make a flogger out of my hair; he said it would feel like nothing in this world. The idea was shocking but intriguing too. Fears of being naked up top battled with the lure of owning an item that would be completely unique.

I stood in the middle of Ash's studio between two doors. The door to the left led to his lab where he kept volatile chemicals, burners and dangerous equipment. The door to the right led outside to the yard. I knew I could leave right now, that I could slip out of the room and make some excuse later that Ash wouldn't believe. I knew he wouldn't push things if I did. I fingered a strand of my long hair and then unbuttoned my coat, submitting to my fate. I shivered, but not from the chill of the December air. Ash kept his studio reasonably warm, so I knew it was nerves that made my skin break out in goose bumps. I stepped out of my shoes and wriggled my bare toes. I was about to pull off my skirt when a loud clang made me jump. The door to Ash's lab opened. My friend poked his head around the corner.

"I'll be out in a bit." He closed the door and then reopened it a moment later. "I'll need you naked, Selma," he called out. "Everything has to come off." The door shut with a bang once more.

I folded my skirt and placed it next to the coat on a chair. I pulled my thick red sweater over my head; it made my hair fall down in disarray. I let my mane spill over my shoulders, tickle my back and flutter below my waist. Twelve years, and my hair had never seen a pair of scissors. Twelve years, and now I was about to let Ash remove it all in a single go. I could hardly imagine myself bald; without my hair, where would I hide?

My lingerie came off as I contemplated a future without my long locks. Removing my silky panties and bra left me finally naked. I still looked like a censored nude: my hair covered my breasts, my belly and the top of my groin. I stood awkwardly on the bare wooden floor, feeling somewhat like a sacrificial lamb. I rubbed the dry skin over my elbows, wishing Lola had told me where to buy her cocoa-butter moisturizer that worked wonders on my skin. I was fidgeting, and I knew it, but I was so nervous, I couldn't keep still. What if Lola had been right? If I lost my hair, became truly naked, would I become a bald, ugly hag? Would I be a freak? I took a deep, calming breath. I could do this. The reward would be worth the effort involved.

Ash came out, startling me by the speed with which he strode across the floor. He wore a long leather apron that made him look like Sweeney Todd. I shuddered at the connection and wished my mind could be still right now. Ash looked me up and down. I squirmed a little beneath his gaze, although he smiled gently at me.

"Relax, Selma."

"I am relaxed."

"I've got some restraints if you like. You can use the handcuffs I made last week."

"Thanks, but no thanks. I'll be fine."

Ash looked at me once more. Through the curtain of my hair I saw him nod.

"I'll make a start then." He fished into a pocket on his apron. He pulled out a large hairbrush. "Kneel."

This was something I could understand, something I was familiar with. Suddenly I didn't feel so scared. A simple order to submit was what I lived for. I folded myself down and knelt on the bare wooden floor. Ash stood behind me. He clutched a handful of my hair, pulling me back roughly. I gasped; the tug was a trigger of pleasure for me. I felt my skin flush with blood as I became aroused. My clit pulsed between my legs, hungry for sensation. I shuddered from my head right down to my toes.

I leaned into Ash's grip, but he stilled my movements.

"Rapunzel," he whispered. "Let down your hair." Ash swept the brush through my locks in a series of long strokes. My hair shone and my heart sang. I was literally purring by the time I counted to fifty. As if in a fog, I heard Ash's voice above me. "Ready?" he asked.

"Yes." I bowed my head as he delved into his pocket once more. This time he held up an oversized rubber band. His hands carefully pulled and stroked my hair into a single ponytail, which he secured efficiently.

I closed my eyes and breathed out, but I refused to look at the next item Ash produced. I knew he held the shears now; I could feel the cold radiate from the metal as it neared my face. I felt like I was waiting for my turn at the guillotine in revolutionary France. My breath froze. I forced myself to swallow, to stay alive long enough to get through this. I listened to the slice of metal, the long snap of razor-sharp blades on my precious hair. *Twelve years,* I thought. Twelve years of length, of feminine beauty that everyone could see. I felt little wisps escape Ash's hands. I wriggled my nose but remained still as he worked quickly. And then I started to feel a lightness, a new weightlessness as Ash stepped away from me. A curl of warm air touched the nape of my neck as he breathed out in relief.

I watched Ash as he stood in front of me. "It should be ready in the morning." I made a move to stand, but Ash stopped me with a raised hand. "Stay there." He disappeared into his lab, only to return with a set of electric clippers. I sat in dazed shock as he dispatched the last remaining strands of my hair. The buzz of the clippers made me shake, and even when he stepped away, smiling with satisfaction, I couldn't stop trembling. He'd taken everything. Something must have shown on my face, because his smile became softer. "Stay tonight."

Ash found a blanket from one of his lockers, and then he lay with me in the middle of the floor; the feel of his clothes on my bare skin made me feel vulnerable, childlike but alive with sensation. I stopped shaking when I curled around his warm bulk. My friend stayed with me until I fell asleep.

As soon as I awoke the next morning, my hand went to my bare scalp. I felt disoriented and confused until I remembered what I had agreed to, what I had given up. Ash was nowhere to be seen.

I wrapped the blanket around me and padded to the small toilet at the side of the building. It was cold out; a wicked chill blew across my skin where the blanket didn't quite cover, but it was my bare head where I felt it the most.

Ash was in the studio when I returned. He had changed his outfit; he now wore a black utility kilt that showed off his hairy legs. "Silly thing," he scolded. "Why didn't you put your clothes back on?"

I was naked without my hair; no amount of fabric would change that. I wanted to tell Ash this interesting fact, but before I could speak, he smiled at me. "It's ready, by the way." He swept a hand from behind his back and held up my hair flogger. "The bond set really well." He twirled it over his head. "What do you think?" Ash passed the flogger to me.

I felt the blanket fall to the floor as I grasped the flogger in my outstretched hands. It was beautiful; a smooth wooden handle held twelve years of my hair that fell in a gentle sweep from the base. I was speechless.

"Would you like to try it now?"

I nodded, aware that my nipples had become erect: the small points ached with need. Ash straightened the blanket on the floor. I lay atop it, my face pressed into the warm pile.

"Rapunzel, Rapunzel," Ash sang. He thrashed down with the flogger in time with his tune. Twelve years of hair touched me, and each strand had its own stinging kiss of pain. It hurt even though it shouldn't have. It hurt a lot. Pleasure gave way to pain, but that led on to yet more pleasure. I felt a sob begin in the back of my throat as he beat me. Ash struck down again with even more force. I had nowhere to hide from his blows. I felt the blood rise to the surface of my back and bottom. My legs parted, my hips twitched. The sensation was too much. I could smell myself, the early morning scent of sweat and desire. I felt ashamed at being such a slut, but the flogger was just perfect. Lola had been right in her own way when she told me a woman's beauty was her hair. The flogger was beautiful, the feelings it stirred up within me were beautiful, and they were mighty powerful, too; I began grinding myself against the blanket, desperate for more. Now that I was truly naked, I could feel every fiber against my skin. It was an amazing experience.

I felt a thud as Ash dropped the flogger next to my face. Soon I felt the rough cotton of his kilt against my backside, the heavy prod of his erection as he rubbed himself all over me. Ash's fingers stroked over my arse and onward to my cunt, where they slipped on my wetness.

"May I?" he asked. He sounded as desperate as I felt.

"Of course." I was granting him a favor, a little something after all he had so graciously given me.

"Selma," he whispered, his voice a reverent supplication.

I felt sparks of power curl inside me from my approaching orgasm; it lifted me from the blanket on the floor. Ash whimpered as his cock moved inside my cunt; each heavy shove was a delightful heaven. I drew him in farther, sucking his power inside me, generating more until I felt like a human dynamo. When Ash came, he kissed my back all over, soothing the places that were sore and hot. I may have been flat on my face, pressed into the blanket, but at that moment, I felt like a goddess, like a temple priestess of the highest order. Ash became my devotee, a man who would worship my body no matter what it looked like, because it would always be beautiful to him.

"I think the Rapunzel flogger is a success," Ash said breathlessly. He rolled off my back to lie at my side.

I thought of other women who used hair for their power. I stroked the flogger and felt twelve years slip through my fingers. "Can we call her Delilah instead?" I asked, my voice a little rough.

"Delilah cut Samson's hair, not the other way around," Ash reminded me as he stroked his fingers over the bare skin of my head.

"But it was hair that held power. It was hair that held strength, whoever wielded it."

Ash picked up my flogger, but I took it from him and clutched it to my breasts. "This is mine now."

Ash held up both hands in a gesture of surrender. "Okay, Delilah it is."

I twirled the flogger in my hand. I smiled as twelve years of hair stroked over my skin. I may have been naked up top, but I was still in possession of my strength.

Ash reached over and ran a finger over my throat. "You're beautiful, you know that?"

"Yeah, I know."

"Good," he said with a grin. "Because naked women turn me on." His lips trailed up my bare neck, over my cheek and to the smooth skin of my scalp. I hummed with pleasure at the feeling, and then I relaxed on the blanket and let him worship me some more.

THE ROYALTON —A DARAY TALE

Tess Danesi

The first snowflakes have chosen today to make their appearance. I leave a trail of footprints in the thin layer of snow that tenaciously sticks to the sidewalk. For a short time, New York will be transformed into a clean and crisp wonderland. I walk a bit more briskly, snow crunching underfoot, careful not to slip in my high-heeled boots. I'm eager to get to the hotel. The doorman, shivering beneath his long black wool overcoat, greets me by name and holds the door open for me. Dar and I have made a habit of visiting the lounge at the Royalton. It's close to both our offices and prior to its recent renovation, was a quiet place to enjoy a cocktail in each other's company at the end of a long day. Now, the new décor has brought new crowds. Evenings after five, it's bustling with trendy New Yorkers, making us sometimes seek the smaller, cozier lounge at the Mansfield, with its library-like ambiance, when we desire less noise amid old world charm. I feel like Mata Hari at the Mansfield, ready to slide a microdot into Dar's waiting palm as we sip Manhattans.

"Stay warm, Tess," says Dean, my favorite doorman, with one final shudder.

"Thanks, you should take that advice yourself, Dean," I reply, wondering if he knows me well enough to sense my anxiety. More likely he thinks it's the cold making me tremble.

It's early; the crowds have not yet arrived, so I select a sofa in a corner, remove my camel cashmere coat, fold it, and place it next to me. I open my bag and remove the envelope Dar had delivered to my office. His instructions were simple.

> *Hello, pet. Be at the Royalton at four. Have one drink, charge it to room 1215. At 4:30 open the sealed envelope, and follow my numbered instructions.*

Like so many times before, I do what Dar requests, though I am tempted to rip open the envelope I now hold in my damp palm. My finger slides along the top edge, my palm presses against the flat surface, as if that will help me intuit what he's written inside. I've been twitchy with anticipation since noon when my assistant brought me the envelope and I read his brief message. I'm thankful that I wore a new dress and pretty new undies today, courtesy of the weekend's Christmas shopping spree. As the waitress brings me my usual Patron, chilled and strained into a frosted martini glass, I think how glad I am that Dar appreciates my near addiction to the accoutrements of femininity. Lace-topped thigh highs and delicate lacy undergarments make him wild. The first sip of the frosty liquid soothes my dry throat and I begin to relax. I know I won't finish my drink, I'm still too nervous, and with Dar it always pays to have my wits about me.

I look at my watch. *Damn the time. It just won't move.* I take another sip of my drink and stare at the envelope I have placed on the table in front of me. I feel the vein in my temple pulsate, indicating how tense I am. *He could simply be planning to take me to dinner*, I think in an effort to center myself. But I know it's more than that. I just wish I had some idea. Then again, I love Dar for many reasons, one of which is his constant ability to take me by surprise. Our relationship is tumultuous. No one has hurt me more, but at the same time, no one had ever made me feel more alive and more treasured than Dar. The price for his love is high; the bruises, more often present than not, on my ass and thighs are tangible manifestations of his sometimes sadistic excesses. But at the same time, no one has stood by me, loved me, and defended me with such vehemence. I often wonder at my ability to fear him and to trust him at the same time.

I glance at my watch and it holds me spellbound. I don't know why I wait for precisely four thirty to arrive. I guess I'm so used to following Dar's directives that I don't even consider how he'd never know if I jumped the gun by ten minutes. So I sit there taking the occasional sip of tequila and fixating on willing the thin silver hands to rotate. Finally, the time arrives and I slide a long cranberry lacquered fingernail under the flap, remove the sheet of Dar's cream-colored stationery, and read the first line. Written in his small, precise handwriting, the first sentence tells me to read and complete each instruction before going on to the next. I feel a familiar tingle between my thighs at the thought of what looks like a long and drawn out evening.

1) Use the enclosed card key and let yourself into room 1215.

I laugh to myself, thinking he should have penned a little stop sign, like those at the end of each section of standardized tests, after each line. It makes me smile as I head for the elevator.

My gaiety is short-lived; the elevator goes directly to twelve and opens. I'm nervous as I make my way down the narrow hallway illuminated only by small sconces and glowing porthole-like lights on each door. Room 1215 looms in front of me and with a mix of excitement and trepidation, I slide the card into the door, then hear a soft click before a pinpoint of green light announces that I may enter. The room has a cool elegance. It's sparsely though expensively furnished in cool tones of metallic gray and rich cream. Decadent linens cover the bed, which is made to look as though it belongs on a cruise ship and can be folded back into the wall. I have no baggage, only my coat and handbag, nothing to busy myself with. I hang up my coat, take the letter out of my bag, and place my purse on the closet shelf. I don't bother to sit before I read the next directive.

> 2) *There's a bottle of Laphroaig on the credenza.*
> *Pour two tumblers and set them on the round glass*
> *table.*

Two glasses of whiskey? My heart is thumping harder than ever. I put my hand on top of my breast, feeling the persistent rhythm against my palm and keeping it there until it slows. Dar knows one of my fantasies has been to be double penetrated by him and another man, but Dar, though he's had his share of kinky three- and more-somes with casual girlfriends, has never shared anyone he cared about deeply. As I pour the amber liquid into the two glasses, inhaling the heavy peaty aroma, I think how Dar has more than satisfied me sexually, awakening a deep and darkly masochistic side of my personality. While I am not submissive in general, I am submissive to him. In the midst of the tidal wave of passion and sadism that is Dar, I never gave much thought to actualizing this particular fantasy. And with Dar's

jealousy, an emotion that has been known to stir up his pro-
found capacity for cruelty, I worry that perhaps it would be best
for all concerned to let it go unrealized. A threesome would explain why I am in this hotel room. This is something Dar would
not want left to linger among the ghosts that haunt his home.
It makes sense to do this here, in a place we can leave behind,
abandoning any specters when we close the door behind us. I
force myself to stop predicting, stop thinking, and look at the
next line.

3) Strip to your bra and panties.

I quickly remove my dress and hang it up neatly in the closet, eager to get to the next instruction. Though I haven't read ahead,
I've seen only a few more are left to go and then I'll be in Dar's
arms. I can't wait. It may not be a warm embrace, I may be
dealing with him in his cool and methodical mood, but to me
just being in his presence is calming. Contradictions abound;
with Dar I feel a deep inner peace even when I am at my most
apprehensive. With Dar there are only extremes: I love him or
I hate him, I feel safe or frightened; often I feel these emotions
at the same time. What is a constant is my fathomless trust in
him. I have a premonition I will be dipping into that well of
faith tonight.

*4) In the dresser drawer there is a blindfold and two
sets of handcuffs. Bring them to the table. Sit in the
middle seat.*

I find the items just as he said; a thick black blindfold and two
sets of steel handcuffs. My body feels as if it's vibrating, the
way a kitten hums as it purrs contentedly in your arms, my cunt

clenching as I hold the cold metal in my hands. I think how tight and unforgiving they'll feel wrapped around my wrists, and wonder if I'll be struggling so that they'll dig into and bruise my thin, delicate flesh. I sit down, my thighs feeling chilled against the frigid aluminum seat, realizing for the first time how cool the room is and knowing that Dar must have turned down the heat. My trembling excites him, be it from the cold or from uncertainty or from fear. I swallow hard, attempting to dislodge the lump in my throat, as I read his final instruction.

> *5) At 5:00, put on the blindfold, put a set of hand-cuffs around both wrists, and secure your left arm to the back rail of the chair. Wait.*

He knows I hate this, that it's not safe to leave me restrained alone, that it will kick in my tendency to panic as my mind turns over all the horrific things that might happen, being in so vulnerable a position. Being in a hotel makes it worse, less predictable. Anyone could walk in. Being scared makes me wet; no one knows that better than Dar.

I know I don't have to do this but I also know that I will. The wetness soaking through my panties and glazing my inner thighs is evidence of how aroused I am despite my nerves. Looking at my watch, I see I only have five minutes to wait. With each minute, my anxiety escalates, and I'm not even restrained yet. I swallow hard against the lump in my throat and force myself to tear my eyes away from my watch. Whatever buzz I had from the drink is gone. Adrenaline flows through my body as I finally settle the blindfold over my eyes, making sure the handcuffs will be easy to reach once my sight is gone. The only noise in the room, the ratcheting sound of the cuffs tightening, competes with the sound of rushing blood in my head.

I don't wait long. Moments later, I hear a card slide into the door and the handle turns. "Hello, pet," he says simply. I reply in the same simple fashion, so nervous and agitated that even saying two words is a struggle. I listen hard to determine if there is anyone else in the room with him, but the thick carpet successfully muffles any sound. I jump when I feel his hand brush my cheek.

"Nervous, pet?" he queries.

"Yes, Dar," I whisper.

"Good," he replies. In my mind I can see the smirk on his handsome face. "You won't be seeing tonight, Tess, at least not until our guest leaves."

My free arm involuntarily covers my breasts at this confirmation that he isn't alone. I squeeze my thighs tightly together in an attempt to subdue the ache in my cunt. Nothing escapes his notice. He pulls my arm away and with a click of the metal sliding home I am utterly helpless.

"Excites you, doesn't it, my beautiful little bitch? Being so helpless, knowing we can do what we will with you?"

Oh, god—we. "Yes."

His breath is hot on my neck. Is it his breath, I suddenly wonder, as I feel him lock the other set of cuffs to the chair?

"I'm giving you what you want tonight, Tess. I'll be buried deep in your ass and another cock will be in that tight, hot cunt of yours. Of course, it will be my way, my rules. You will never know who it is touching you, whose cock you're gagging on. Does that suit you?"

I nod my head; my throat feels too dry to answer. Suddenly, warmth spreads through my face as his palm connects hard with my cheek.

"Answer me, bitch."

"Daray, please, please just tell me..." I start, beginning to panic at the thought that he might have invited a stranger. It disturbs me so much I use his full name to get his attention. I've always imagined this scene happening naturally, the result of an evening of comfortable companionship among friends and maybe a bit too much alcohol.

He reads my mind, he always does. How he does it I'll never know. I wish I could look into his eyes and see his thoughts with a modicum of the success he has at deciphering mine. As he leans into me, I picture him bending his long, muscular frame over the back of the chair as his rough cheek is pressed to my smooth, heated face. "Do you think I'd allow a stranger to touch you, pet? Tsk. Now be a good girl, no more questions."

"Have a seat," he says to the hushed presence.

Glasses clink as I picture them sitting there. Are they looking at me, appraising me? Are they ignoring me, content to sip their whiskey in silence? Time loses meaning and I begin to fidget in my seat. It might have been five minutes or twenty when I feel the chair being pushed back away from the table and strong hands roughly pull my breasts from my bra. I gasp and Dar quiets me. Warm liquid spills from my shoulders, over my breasts, down my belly and pools on the aluminum seat, mingling with the slick fluid that coats my sex and thighs. My senses are overwhelmed by the intense smoky aroma when a tongue starts to lick my neck slowly, so damn slowly, making its way down the gentle slope of my breast. My nipple is sucked into a hot mouth. Whose, I wonder? Then it doesn't matter as I feel the heat of another tongue following the same erotic path on the other side. My head rolls back as I revel in this decadent sensation. Teeth bite into one nipple, pulling and stretching it while the other mouth remains soft and supple on my breast. The conflicting sensations keep me even more on edge. I feel intoxicated as both tongues begin to move down my sides and lap up the liquid that has accumulated in the crease of my thighs. Teeth bite into the tender flesh of my inner thigh. The heat of a tongue pressed against the sheer scrap of fabric that barely covers my pussy makes me push myself greedily against whoever's mouth it is. I realize I don't care—I just don't want it to stop.

I lose the attention of one mouth as the handcuffs that restrain me are removed. I know the mouth that continues to press against my cunt isn't Dar's. Only Dar would have the keys. *Oh, god, oh, god*, I think, too lost in these moments to worry about Dar's reaction. Whatever will be will be as long as I continue to surrender myself to Dar and the moment. I'm pulled up from my seat, my bra removed, panties slid down my thighs until they puddle at my ankles.

"Step out," Dar says.

I do and I'm naked in front of my lover and this mysterious male presence. Given a moment to think, I wonder who this could be. I don't wonder for long. I'm pushed back onto the corner of the bed. Placed so that my cunt is available at one end and my head hangs off the other side. A cock is at my lips and I open eagerly to take it in. A male groan fills the room as it slides over my lips, into the velvety softness of my mouth, and down my throat. Hands spread my legs farther. I feel like a plaything, having no say in what gets done to me, a feeling I'm not sure I enjoy on a conscious level but here, now, while my clit is sucked into that mouth, pulled at, bitten, coaxed out of hiding, until it feels twice its normal size, and a rigid cock is fucking my face, there is no right and wrong, only pleasure. Sensations that carry me away until I feel myself slide over the edge and I'm bucking wildly against the face between my thighs, wanting to scream as I come but unable to because that cock is relentlessly pumping into my open mouth.

I want to know who is where but the silence of the men, except for grunts and moans, makes it impossible. Dar only talks when he wants me to know precisely where he is. I hope at one point he'll slip up but given his amazing level of self-control, I know that's unlikely. It seems the other man has taken a temporary vow of silence. Suddenly my mouth is empty; a hand surrounds my narrow wrist and pulls me into position.

I'm on top of someone. He lies flat underneath me and I think of letting my hands run down along his belly, wondering if that would give me an indication of who I am on top of. Before I can do anything, someone is behind me, his erect cock pressed against my ass. Hands are everywhere—alternately squeezing then slapping my breasts, spreading my ass. Fingers slide into my cunt and my ass, hands entwine in my hair. I'm floating yet grounded as the cock that is to claim my cunt impales me, taking my breath away for a moment. "Oh, fuck, oh, god, yes," I hear myself say and then I go silent as cool liquid is poured on and rubbed into my asshole.

"Relax, pet," Dar whispers into my ear. I'm comforted to know it's him behind me, his magnificent cock about to slide into my ass. Dar is big and thick, and the cock in my pussy now feels much the same; it fills me completely, making it hard to imagine it possible to have another cock inside me, even in another hole, at the same time.

The head of his cock prods my tight bud. He stops and takes a moment to use his fingers, adding more lube, stretching me slowly to prepare me. I almost cry; for Dar this is a display of tenderness. His breath warms my neck as he whispers more encouraging words in my ear. "Shhh, Tess, shhh," he says soothingly, even as the head of his cock pushes past my tense muscles, making me scream in an alien voice not mine, too feral to be coming from me. He takes a moment, kissing my neck, nuzzling my earlobes before pushing his entire length in. It's insanely intense; there are no words, what words would do? Only three rapidly beating hearts, three sweat-glazed bodies together in a primal bond, moaning and panting their pleasure as they move in rhythm.

As the movements get harder, more intense, Dar reverts to his harsher self, pulling my hair so hard my neck hurts, biting painfully into my shoulder, making me scream so loud for a moment I worry about people in the next room or hallway hearing us. His words are harsher as well. "Is this what you wanted, bitch? You love it, don't you, my little whore? Can't get enough cock. Is this enough for you? Is it?"

"Yes. Oh, god, yes," I shout. I'm surprised I can even speak with the intensity of this new sensation. I can feel their cocks touch through the thin wall separating my cunt from my ass. I know they must feel each other too and it makes me even crazier. I realize this must be someone Dar knows well and trusts implicitly. There is only one person I can think of who fits that bill, and who is so similar in body type that it would be difficult to tell them apart without my sight: Jack, his best friend, the bastard who has always disliked me. Dar claims it's simply because Jack is protective. I find it nearly impossible to believe that anyone would think Dar needs protecting, but at the same time I am begrudgingly grateful that Dar has so loyal a friend.

My thoughts vanish as they both pump harder into me. I'm going to come, I can't help myself, it's too much, too intense, I want it to continue forever, and I want it to stop immediately. There is no more rhyme or reason to my thoughts. I'm crazed, lost in a mad eddy of sensation and emotion when spasms rock my body. My cunt tightens, strangling the heavy cock inside me, my ass pulsating hard around Dar's cock. I hear a low groan, and the hand stiffens in my hair; Dar pulls out of my ass and roars as his come warms my back and flows, dripping in thick rivulets, to coat my ass. He continues holding me, helping to lift and lower me on the cock still enveloped inside me.

"Come again," he says in that voice that broaches no argument. "Come for me, slut. Come with that cock inside and my hands on your throat."

When he moves his large hands to my throat, I inhale deeply, tightening every muscle in my body in anticipation of losing my breath for seconds that I know from experience will feel like hours. But he doesn't squeeze, he just presses firmly, allowing me my breath, though making me aware it's in his power to take it away as he pleases. My orgasm builds rapidly with the combination of his words, his firm hands, and the stiff cock pounding me hard enough to bump my cervix. As I come again I feel the man underneath me slam into me one final time. "Jesus fucking Christ," he exclaims. "Jesus Christ." I'm sure the words were unintentional but impossible to be restrained. Just those five words confirm that it is Jack. And as soon as I think that, I begin to doubt myself. At least I think it's him. I wonder if I'll ever be sure.

Dar lifts my limp body up and places me gently on the bed. I feel the bed shift as they both get up and then hushed whispers, words I can't make out. Water starts running in the bathroom. I want to get up and take off this damn blindfold, but I don't dare. I'm elated that Dar has made this fantasy come true for me. I know with his protectiveness and possessiveness, it couldn't have been easy for him. I wonder what, if any, price I'll have to pay. Then I laugh to myself, remembering one of Dar's rules—there is always a price to pay.

There are more whispers and finally the sound of the door opening and closing. The ghost has gone. I picture him vanishing, dissolving into mist before he even reaches the elevator, a phantom that will haunt the halls of this hotel forever. Dar tells me he's going to dim the lights. Then he walks to the bed, pulls me up to my knees, and slides the blindfold off. Even though the room isn't bright, I blink a few times as my eyes grow accustomed to sight. Then all I see are his deep brown eyes. I'm staring at him, trying to access his thoughts, his mood, when he smiles that devilish grin, halfway between a sneer and a smile. He's standing in front of me, naked, still with the glow of sex evident in the sheen on his body, his cock semierect.

"My trousers are on the chair. Go and bring me the belt from them, pet," he says. He doesn't take his eyes from mine until I walk past him on my way to do his bidding. "You can reimburse me with tears, Tess. I think that will do for now."

Ah, I think, a smile he can't see stretching across my face as I feel my own excitement start to build again, *that is a price I am more than willing to pay.*

THE SUN IS AN ORDINARY STAR

Shanna Germain

He was cleaning the bedroom for Stella's return when he heard it. He'd been down on his haunches, swishing the broom beneath the bed's dark corners, when something metallic clanked against the broom. He fished it out.

There, among the dust bunnies and dirt, was Stella's favorite set of nipple clamps, two silver clips connected by a thin chain. The metal was dusty and a few of Stella's long hairs were wound in the chain. Still on his haunches, he picked the clamps up. They were lighter than he remembered, more fragile, the weight of them in his palm almost nothing.

He opened one of the large clips, ran his finger across the row of teeth. Croc heads, Stella called them. Before everything, she'd call home from the office some days, leave a message on the machine. "You're going to have to get out the crocs tonight," she'd say.

Last time she'd called home was right before Christmas. She'd been working on the big holiday shoe campaign, Photoshopping sweat and muscles and boobs onto famous athletes. Even on the message her voice was shaky. "Baby, I'm not feeling up to par," she said. "Let's get those alligator maws out tonight. And whatever else you can think of. I know you're gonna make me feel better."

And he had. As soon as she'd walked in the door, still in her cream-colored work pants and the brown blouse that matched her eyes, her long dark hair pulled back, he'd ordered her to undress. She looked tired, light gray circles under her big brown eyes, but she'd asked and he always tried to give her what she asked for. He'd ordered her to undress him, too, and then he'd cuffed her arms to their slatted headboard. She was pale curves against the purple bedspread. Her long hair, loose from its clip, waved out around her head.

With her arms above her head, her small tits tilted upward. He loved her tits, pale and down-fuzzed as summer peaches, but it was her nipples that he loved the most, the way they stretched high and taut when she was aroused. He'd teased her first, rubbing the sharp edge of the clamp teeth along the inside of her thigh, around the edges of her neck, in smaller and smaller circles around her nipples. He loved to watch the points push into her skin.

Stella was as still as he'd told her to be, mouth closed, only her flared nostrils giving away her arousal. When he saw she was wet, he slid the opened clamp along the edge of her pussy lips, up to her clit. He'd never clamped her there, but he'd promised her it was coming. Now he closed the clamp, just a bit, on that pale pink flesh. She arched her back and gasped.

He took the clamps away, slapped the curvy bottom of her ass, hard enough to feel the sting on his palm. "Be still," he said.

She closed her eyes, her nostrils flaring. When her eyes were closed, he opened both clamps and then closed them on the rosy skin of her nipples. Stella inhaled deeply through her nose.

He leaned back and watched her, the metal clips closed onto her taut flesh, leaving little pinpoints of bloodless skin. At the end of the bed, Stella's feet, the only thing she couldn't keep still, arched in their bonds. Her clit was aching, he knew. "You want to be fucked?" he asked.

Stella knew enough to keep quiet, even to shake her head a little from side to side.

He put one finger inside the hot wetness of her, curled it into an arch. "No?" he asked.

"No," she said. But her pussy gave her away, the way she stretched against her bonds to take more of his finger inside her. He entered her with a second finger.

"You're sure?" he asked. He loved to watch her at this moment. His Stella, stubborn as her Aries sign, truth-speaking, Type A. The internal struggle—to say what she wanted, to take what she wanted, or to give up to him, just for these few moments. This, he knew, was why she wanted to be topped, needed to be topped. This was why he loved it. His cock loved it too, of course, but his mind loved to get her here, to this final release.

He wriggled his fingers inside her, hard against her walls. "I'm sorry, what?" he said, even though she hadn't said anything.

"No," she breathed. Just once. But he knew it was enough. He took his fingers out. "Look at me," he said. And she did, while he entered her, his cock going deep inside her and one hand pulling the nipple clamps, hard and harder, until she begged to be let loose.

He reached up and unbuckled the cuffs. "One hand on your clit." She did as he said, she put one hand on her clit, two fingers rubbing furiously back and forth. The sight of her was almost enough to make him come.

He entered her again, keeping himself back far enough that she could still work her clit. Her other hand reached for something to hold on to. "The clamps," he said. "Pull."

And she did, pulling her nipples up and up with the chain, arching her back to press her clit into him and her hand. He came before she did, but was hard enough to keep inside until she came. Her orgasm was soft, quiet moans and one last tug on the clamps.

He eased himself out of her, and sat beside her on the bed. When he took the clamps from her nipples, she moaned again, turning her head away. He kissed her nipples gently. She turned back toward him, her brown eyes no longer squinted-up from stress. She still looked tired though, beneath her eyes and around the edges of her lips. He stroked her hair and she snuggled her face into the curve of his neck. "You always know exactly what I need," she said. And then she'd fallen asleep, her breath soft and quiet against his skin.

That was six weeks, two surgeries, and some kind of newfangled chemo ago. Today, Stella was coming home. He didn't know what to do with the clamps, and he couldn't bear to touch the cold metal any longer, so he opened the nightstand drawer.

The books from friends and family—*Coping with Cancer, Outsmart Your Cancer, Cancer Husband*—stared up at him, spines uncracked. He'd tried to read the *Husband* one during one of Stella's appointments, but he hadn't understood what was about to happen, and the chapters on lumpectomy and chemo and sex with cancer had seemed impossible. Now, he wished he'd read it, at least the sex chapter, although he doubted there was anything about the kind of sex he and Stella had. *Used* to have. They'd had sex once or twice while she was sick, but it had been the kind of soft, gentle sex he'd always imagined belonged to virgins and old people. When Stella's bones hurt after hot showers and she couldn't sleep because the sheets tore at her skin, they'd fallen into this habit of moving quietly together, him raising himself above her, cock and pussy the only place they touched. And then even that had fallen away, forgotten under the bed in the midst of doctors and options and books and Stella's determination.

Stella had tackled cancer the same way she tackled a big project at work, or, when he'd first met her, a research paper in grad school. Learn the facts, make a to-do list, and then checkmark your way down to the end. Get diagnosed, check. Find the best doctor they could afford, check. Explore all the treatments, check. Get rid of it, check. He didn't want to admit it, but Stella had handled all this with her usual grace and determination, while he was the one who felt lost.

Now, they had cut it out of her body, and she was coming home to him. And he felt like the world's biggest asshole for what he wanted. Or the world's whiniest husband: *My wife went to Cancerville and all I got was this stupid T-shirt.* He wanted her down on her knees, the gorgeous globes of her ass pink-marked, begging him for mercy. He wanted to tie her up and enter her, one half-inch at a time, until she bucked her hips against him. He wanted to clamp the clips in his hand around the points of her nipples and force her to fuck herself until she came, until the tightness left her body and she could fall asleep again, at the point of his neck, without worry. He wanted to give her that release, but without topping her, without hurting a body that had already been beaten by its own cells, but he didn't know how.

Simply the possibility of it made his cock harden. He reached down to rub himself through his pants, and then he realized he was still holding the nipple clamps. Shiny guilt-makers. He dropped them onto the pile of books and shut the drawer tight. It was almost time to pick Stella up anyway.

Stella came home from the hospital with a new pair of reading glasses and a new star, dark red against her pale skin. He saw the glasses as soon as she got in the car—she put the blue- and yellow-striped frames on so she could see the street signs, even though she wasn't driving. He hadn't seen the star yet, but he felt it radiating from her body, sending heat through her white T-shirt, through the blue fleece she wore over it, through the shawl she had wrapped around her shoulders. The heat made him feel like he'd landed on the surface of some unknown sun. Sweat started at the edges of his hairline.

In the seat beside him, Stella shivered. He took his hand off the window button.

"Temperature okay?" he asked. She turned from the window. Her now-short hair was peppered with early gray above her ears. The pinkish tint of the glasses turned her brown eyes toward black, made the purple half-moons beneath her eyes even darker.

"It's fine," Stella said. "Thank you."

Her voice sounded like a grandmother's, soft and sugar-sweet. In fact, everything about her screamed "grandmother": the half-sized glasses, the way she held onto the seatbelt with one bird-bone hand, the slow sighs that she didn't even know she was making. Still, she held herself straight up in her seat, not allowing her head to lean on the seat rest.

"Your mom bring the glasses?" he asked, to hear her speak instead of sigh.

Stella touched the earpiece as though she'd forgotten she had them on. "I rang a nurse," she said. She took the glasses off and folded them. "Had them brought up from the gift shop. My vision's gone haywire."

Stella had her head back at the window. He watched her while he drove. The disease had tightened her round face, made her cheekbones seem higher and larger. His instinct was to reach between the seats and take her hand. Reassure her: *They got it all, everything's fine.* But he couldn't stand to see her turn back toward him, to see her eyes hidden behind the lenses.

But she surprised him by reaching her hand out to his across the space. He took it, even though he needed to shift. He didn't understand much about what was happening or why, but he understood that you didn't waste time and you didn't turn down an extended hand. Her hand felt light and empty, a discarded crab shell.

With her other hand, Stella rubbed at something on the window. "I'm tired," she said. It seemed to be the beginning of a sentence. He waited, her hand lighter and lighter in his own. The only sound was the rev of the unshifted car and the squeak of Stella's finger against the window. These sounds stretched out so long he thought he might have misjudged, maybe there wasn't more she wanted to say. He let his foot farther off the gas—they were going 20 in a 40 now—and opened his mouth.

Stella tightened her fingers on his. "I'm tired," she said again. "But I was thinking ..." she broke off, rubbed the window harder. A car came up behind them, blinked its lights. He shifted the wheel to the right, gave them space to go around. His ears felt like they were the only thing alive, listening for her.

She looked at him finally, gave him a smile that didn't show her teeth. Her fingers unraveled from his. "You should shift," she said. He did, and the car gave a grateful lurch ahead. They drove in silence the rest of the way home, Stella's soft-shell hands holding tight to her seatbelt.

That night, he was surprised when Stella got into bed next to him in only a T-shirt. He'd picked up *Cancer Husband*, and found it wasn't that bad, if a little froufrou for his taste. Of course, he'd started with the chapter on sex. Very vanilla, but still.

Stella reached out and took the book from his hands. She closed it without letting him mark his place and dropped it on the floor beside the bed.

"No more reading," she said.

Hearing her say that made him smile. She used to say that all the time, when she wanted his attention for cuddling, for sex. He rolled toward her. Her body took up less space now—still her, only smaller, as if she'd been slightly shrunk. Still the same curves, the waist that hollowed out toward her round hips. He felt huge next to her, a dangerous giant who might roll over and crush her.

He couldn't resist her play. He put his hand soft against her arm, slid it up beneath the shirt sleeve. Her skin was cool, but for the first time in a long time, her muscles didn't tighten in pain at his touch.

"No more reading?" he said. "Why, do you have something better for me to do?"

Stella put her nose against his neck, inhaled deep.

"I might be able to think of something," she said.

He swallowed hard, unable to speak. How does it feel when your wife comes on to you, finally, finally, after cancer? You feel like the earth has been out of axis, but you didn't notice, until just now, when everything rights itself and settles in, the way it's supposed to be.

"I've missed your body," she said. A sigh, but different from the sighs she'd made in the car. "I've missed *my* body."

How to say he'd missed her body too? He didn't know, so he answered with his fingers on the curve of her hip, followed the slimmed half-circle of her ass. No underwear. The crease where the bottom of her ass met her legs was soft and smooth. Just the feel of it made his hand ache to slap it.

He almost did slap her, but took his hand away, fisted it around the blanket. How could he even think of it? He didn't know, couldn't imagine what kind of person he was to want it the way he did.

Stella's lips moved smooth against his neck. She took his hand from the blankets, but laid it back on the edge of her hip, where her T-shirt met her skin.

"Undress me," she said.

She sat up, and he pulled her shirt off over her head. And there was her star, right above her right nipple, the red heat of it dulled. He wanted to put his finger on it, to lick it and taste it like sun-warmed earth. He thought it would burn his tongue.

He said, "Does it hurt?"

"Stop asking," she said, and her voice was brisk, but also tired.

He nodded. Even to himself, he'd started to sound like a quiz book. How are you? What do you need? How do you feel? It was as if he didn't know what to say when he wasn't asking about her. He searched for something about his own day that would be interesting to her. *I thought about fucking you the way we used to. I thought about clamping your nipples until you cried, until you could sleep and smile again.*

Stella put her own finger over the star, pressed harder than he would have thought.

"Sometimes it hurts," she said. "Not now."

She dropped her hands, put them on his hips.

"Anyway, I don't want to think about it," she said. "Can you just fuck me?"

Her voice was beyond Type A into bitter, a spit of bad tastes.

It hardened his cock and made him nervous to touch her, at the same time. She closed her eyes and leaned her head back, exposing the full length of her soft, white neck, the pulse that talked to him there. He leaned into the pulse, put his lips against the thin blue line.

"Yes," he said. "I can fuck you."

But, then, he couldn't. He wanted to, he tried, but the star kept shining up at him off her skin, a beacon to remind him. Everything he did—his tongue at her pink nipples, avoiding the scar, his fingers down her pale belly, even the moment when, finally, he entered her, every ounce of him, his entire cock, inside her—at every moment he was making love, he was taking care. He didn't realize it at the time, he thought they were together in this slow, languid night. But right before he came, he opened his eyes and saw her looking somewhere else. Her body moved in the slow-motion rhythm he'd started, but her mouth made small noises of pain. He tried to rise up off her, but he was already coming, too late to stop, and his shudders made his "I'm sorry"s sound tinny and hollow, as if they were coming from light years away.

Stella didn't come on to him again. He wasn't surprised, but he still hoped for it, watched for her to take the lead when she felt okay, but there was nothing. She didn't even undress in front of him.

Within the week, Stella started work again, and they settled back into what he thought of, sadly, as their old rhythm: too much work-work and house-work, passing each other on the stairs or in the kitchen, hands full of laundry or dinner. He'd thought that once someone got sick, the way Stella had been sick, you didn't, couldn't, just go back to normal. That you never took life for granted, or passed each other in the hallway without touching.

He started masturbating in the shower. One hand on his cock, the other against the shower door, in case she came in to pee. He was embarrassed for himself, for his desire, but he didn't want to embarrass her, or make her feel worse. He used Stella's soap—it smelled of sage, which smelled of her—lathering it until he could slide his fist up and down. Although he tried to think of other things, his mind was all Stella, Stella in nipple clamps, her ass beneath the flat of his hand. Keeping quiet, coming with Stella in the house but without her, made his teeth ache and the bottom of his stomach clench up in cramps. And, still, he couldn't stop. The pain cleansed him somehow, made it safe for him to be around her.

But after two weeks, he couldn't stand not touching her anymore. He put his arms around her one morning while she was dressing and kissed the bare back of her neck. The smell of her sage soap and her curves against the fabric of her skirt made him press his hips into her ass, harder than he'd meant to.

Stella leaned against him, bare shoulder blades into his chest. She let her head fall back onto his shoulder, and he kissed the side of her mouth. He hadn't realized how much he'd missed her breath, minty and sweet.

"You'll make me late for work," she said against his lips.

"Do you care?" he asked.

She shook her head no, and he turned her toward him, pressed his mouth hard to hers. His hands followed her lower back down to her ass. He cupped his palms around her curves and pulled her hard against him.

Stella made a small cry into his mouth. Panic spread up through his chest. He let go of her body, stepped back.

"Jesus, Stella, I'm sorry," he said. But even in his panic over hurting her, he couldn't stop looking at her body. How her nipples were like stars too, a constellation against the sky of her chest. How her waist curved in and then swelled into hips. His cock twitched, sending a mixed flood of arousal and shame. Worst husband of the year award, right here.

"Don't you dare," she said. Her voice was shaky, something he hadn't heard before. "Don't you fucking dare tell me one more time how sorry you are," she said.

He nodded. His body was heavy, heavy. His hands, his head, his cock shrinking against his thigh, everything held on the bed by this strange gravity. He vowed he would masturbate every day, he would take a lover if he had to. He would not ask anything more of Stella, of her body, than what she offered him.

Stella stepped closer to where he sat. And there was her star, shining with its red heat. He couldn't look away. Did his eyes feel pain? He thought they might.

"Touch it," she said.

But he couldn't until she took his wrist and brought his fingers to her skin. The star wasn't hot at all. It felt like Stella's skin, only more so. Thicker, tougher, with six small rays leading out. And she didn't flinch when he pushed a bit against the small points of it. Instead, he thought she might be leaning into him harder.

He pulled his finger away, looked down at it in his lap. Did the tip of it burn, or was it only his guilt that made the skin seem hot? He couldn't tell.

"I don't know what to do," he said.

Stella put her hands beneath her breasts, lifted them up, her nipples pink stars in their own right. His cock tried to stir, but stayed down beneath the weight of air.

"I need you—" Stella started, and then got down on her knees in front of him. There was no rug, and he worried about her knees on the hardwood, but she didn't seem to notice.

"I can only say this once," she said. "Maybe, maybe I can't say it at all."

When Stella tried not to cry, her nose pinkened at the edges. It didn't happen often. He'd seen it once, maybe twice, since he'd known her. The splotches of pink made him happy, not because he wanted her to cry, but because he suddenly felt less alone in this thing that had happened.

Stella covered his hands with her own, then lifted her chin until her brown eyes looked right into his.

"I need you to stop fucking me like I'm dying," she said, and her lips moved fast, like she was afraid they would stop. "I'm not dying. But every time you touch me soft, every time you ask if I'm okay, another little piece of me falls off."

Something started within him, a pain he had not known. It began at the inside of his chest, flowed outward to his skin, his arms. His breath hitched and came ragged. He wondered if he was having a heart attack. He squeezed Stella's hands, and she squeezed back.

"Now," she said, "I'm going to walk out of the room, and when I come back, I need you to fuck me like I'm actually alive."

Then she stood and turned. Still stuck to the bed, unable to rise or move, he watched her walk out of the room, the strength of her bare back, the way her ass filled out her skirt. The star he couldn't see, but could still feel, not as heat, but as light, guiding him.

"Baby," she said and her voice was strong and sure from out in the hallway, "You're going to have to get out the crocs today."

At the sound of her voice, his body came free of the gravity that held it. He could raise his hands, stand. His cock, too, rose as high as it could beneath his jeans. Before she came back in, he pulled open the nightstand and dug the nipple clamps from beneath the stack of books they didn't need to read. He looked at the clamps in his hands, their pointy teeth, and remembered the contrast their silver shine made against Stella's skin. The way she sighed in release when he clamped them to her nipples. He smiled and slid the clamps beneath the pillow for later. Let her think he'd forgotten, let her wonder. He was the one in charge, after all.

She walked in, naked now, her star shining from its place on her chest. He moved toward her, following its light.

BELTED

Rachel Kramer Bussel

You'd never know the belt is there by looking at him. It's lost between his shirt and his pants, tucked away, hidden, pulled close, serving a dual purpose. You'd never know it's there, unless he made a point of showing you. And he does, often, a hand resting there as a reminder in public, an intimation of what will happen in private. You have no idea how many other girls he makes a point of showing it to, but the reason you keep returning is that when you're with him, you don't care about the other girls. There could be hundreds, thousands even; as long as he looks at you the way he does when he unbuckles and unfurls the soft, worn, brown leather, then coils the belt purposefully around his hand, you can let yourself believe he wears it just for you.

This isn't the first belt that's been used to strike you. There was the boyfriend in college who had you bend over, skirt around your ankles, camera flashing and belt lashing against your skin before plunging his oversized cock into your unprepared ass. He was all flash and no finesse.

Your lover is the opposite, or rather, flash and finesse mixed together in a dizzying way, with plenty of substance to back them up. He holds the belt like it belongs in his hand, like it's an extension of him. He tells you that he thinks about you every day when he loops it through his pants, when he touches the cool metal buckle. Alone in some room or another—never either of your bedrooms—your body reacts before you have time to consider its wisdom when you see him reaching for the buckle. After all, you know from experience that could mean anything—he's giving you his cock to suck, he's going to shackle your arms behind your back, he's going to pull your hair hard and slap your face until you cry, he's going to beat you until your skin is heated from the outside in. All of these are possibilities, and all of these bring you pleasure, but you hope it's the latter.

The belt is able to speak in ways that even the both of you, wordsmiths by trade, cannot always do. The belt is not a "toy" for "foreplay" but a separate part of your sex life, one that may appear at any moment. Its presence lurks while you casually sip your drinks at the bar, hidden but powerful; your fingers are itching to stroke it, if only so they can be slapped away. You never know if he will bring it out, how he will use it, how much of the belt and himself he will give you.

You try not to be greedy, but you hope it'll be a moment like this: You're sore from having his cock inside you, from him holding you down, from his hand crushing your neck. Sore in a good way, so you almost don't even miss the belt—almost. You never have much time, can never stay overnight, have to steal hours out of other people's schedules to accommodate this affair, so you learn to take what you can get. You're wondering when he will have to leave, when this spell of lust will fade back into real life, when he reaches for the belt from the floor. "Turn over," he tells you, and you roll onto your stomach, your pale backside before him.

Your face is turned away from him, sunken into the softness of the pillow, freshly washed hair now tousled and messy. The tip of the belt rests against your newly shaved lips as you hear the words, "Spread your legs." You do, because you always do, because this is what your relationship is about: he orders, you obey, and you both like it like that. Your hands instinctively curl around the pillow, long nails digging into the cotton and feathers as you wait. The belt strikes the air and you shiver, feeling a breeze that may be a phantom one or may be very, very real. The next sound you hear coincides with a strike of the belt on your cheeks, both of them, a slice that takes a moment to process before you say the words almost automatically: "Thank you."

There's never a "You're welcome," or rather, not a verbal one. It's implied by the next stinging strike, by the fact that you're deemed worthy at all. He doesn't talk then, is almost solemn as you wait for it to be over with equal parts dread and glee.

But those kinds of smacks aren't what make you come. No, that's saved for when he makes you cry. You turn over and open your eyes for a moment to look at him, hovering over you. You marvel that you can feel so close when he's not touching you with his body at all. The belt is capable of magic. You start to shiver once you realize what's going to happen, that the belt is not just teasing your lips with a kiss, though you pucker up when it approaches.

Then the belt moves on to its real work, kissing your other set of lips harder, the equivalent of a shove-you-against-the-wall, bruising kiss. This kiss is merely an introduction, a warm-up. You know what's coming and even though you want it, you press your legs together involuntarily until he barks at you to put them back. You shut your eyes because you know you can't watch this. Your hands are twisted above your head, clinging to each other for some kinky version of safety. You focus on keeping your legs open, all of you exposed. When the belt strikes there, right there, you don't quite scream; it's more of a strangled, garbled cry. Your hand automatically goes to cover the sting, to cradle yourself. You finally get a "Good girl."

You try to turn over, to curl into a ball, but you're not allowed, or rather, your desire to prove yourself wins out over your desire to stop what's coming. You didn't travel for hours just to shy away from the pain. But you almost forget that when the next blow strikes. You wonder how the tender skin between your legs can stand that force, and then you stop wondering when the belt moves upward, to your breasts, your pebbled nipples no match for the blows. You arch your back and thrust upward, even though inside, you want to cower. You reluctantly remember telling him you wanted bruises there, marks you could proudly reveal with a hint of cleavage, a well-timed reveal as you lean over on the train. You still want the marks but breathe deep through your nose, twist your fingers more tightly around each other, to get through them. You bite your lip as the sweet pain of the belt heats your chest and wanders downward. You almost get used to the rhythm, your nipples stubbornly rising after each blow.

Then it's back down, back to the place that no longer feels like your cunt, not the way it's being set afire again and again. These lashes aren't as swift as the ones against your breasts, but they are sure, steady. He's not twice your size for no reason, and each slap strikes precisely where he wants it to. The tears finally appear in the form of sobs, traveling fast through your body, a current of energy you use to sustain yourself through the last few lashes. You'd think the pain would be a little more subdued, the pussy's diminishing law of returns, but no. You feel every ounce of force he uses for each stroke, every bite of the leather into your inner thighs, against your wetness. You have a vision of the belt wrapped around your throat, the buckle cold against your skin as you stare deep into his eyes, but that was another time, another place. The next blow has you thrashing so much he has to hold you down.

Is it the belt that makes you come? The leather, the thrash, the pain, the jolt? Is it the force behind it? Is it the noises he makes as he does it, the hitches of breath that are nothing like your shuddering sobs but are music to your ears nonetheless—is that what makes you finally go over the edge? Is it him holding you down, him promising you pain that may or may not come?

Maybe it's all of it, all the forces combining to make the orgasm nothing like what you were expecting, the kind where your body bonds with the belt, giving back some of its life force, only to have it beaten back into you. Though you know that logically, rationally, it's impossible, you hope the belt has absorbed some of your tears, has taken them and held on to them for next time, has put the pain that you mostly wanted, but kind of didn't, somewhere for safekeeping, somewhere he can hold next to his skin any time he desires.

Oh, it's not like you really have time to think all that or think anything, not then. The belt is reminding you, lash by lash, that you must stay open, stay ready, stay through the moments when you don't know how you will get through it, stay through the times you don't have a chance to take a bracing breath or perform any other magic tricks to turn the pain into something else. By now even the light touches, the strokes of the belt's rough edge against your fleshy inner thigh, the dance of the musky leather against your cheek, are enough to make you shudder, like when he raises his hand to smack you but stops right before his fingers reach the finish line. The effect is the same.

You breathe through your nose, a more refined type of breath, one granted you by the momentary lapse before the belt is between your legs again, crashing hard, calling forth wetness you didn't know you still had. Pain, pleasure, obedience, pride, love, hate, fear ride each other along the waves of your body until you hardly know who you are anymore. You've moved beyond some simple goal of taking it into somewhere else, somewhere you're afraid to look at too closely lest it prove to be just a mirage.

And then, almost too fast, it's over. The belt lies limp on the bed and you're allowed to press your legs together again, to admire the bruises on your chest that you will wind up keeping close like a secret. You wipe the tears from your cheeks, embarrassed but secretly pleased. What happens after that hardly even matters, because that is what will remain, not the belt or the pain or the marks, but the beauty of being transformed by each of them into someone new, blossoming like the bruises on and under your skin; traveling with him somewhere far away, somewhere magical no one else will ever visit, where each strike of the belt serves to bind you together in this sensual cocoon, sealing you in with its heat long after the physical marks drift away.

You hope it'll be something like that, but with him, you never know what you're going to get, and you wouldn't have it any other way.

LUNCH

Elizabeth Coldwell

It's five to twelve, and I am waiting for his email. Like every other day, it will come on the dot of midday, and like every other day, it will tell me what I can have for lunch and where I can eat it. If I have been good—and I always think I have, because I try so hard to live up to the standards Michael sets for me—I might be allowed to go and sit in the sandwich bar across the road with Jo and Carly and have a mochaccino and a slice of carrot cake with cream cheese icing. If I have been bad, then I will have to sit on my own in my office, picking at a boring green salad. It's a ritual that has existed between us for almost a year now, and it has come to define the way our relationship has developed since the moment I first realized I like it when he takes control.

I've never explained to anyone why my eating arrangements vary so much from day to day. Mention that my husband is telling me what to do, and people will be expecting me to walk in one morning with bruises on my face and the excuse that I walked into a door. Say that it's a domination game and they'll peg us as a couple of sickos into whips and chains and all manner of unspeakable acts. So I make some comment about work piling up and not having the time to leave my desk, or let everyone think I'm on the latest diet from the pages of a glossy magazine. After all, how many of the women here don't have some strange, self-inflicted restrictions on what they eat, whether that's cutting out meat and dairy, passing on the carbs, or existing on nothing but coffee, cigarettes and fresh air?

Still, I shouldn't have to worry about any of that today—or so I think. And then the mail icon is bouncing insistently at the bottom of my screen, and I know his instructions have arrived. I click on the message and scan his words. *Sorry, no date with the girls today. If you'd wanted a treat, you should have remembered to pick up my gray suit from the dry cleaner's.* Guiltily, I slide open the top drawer of my desk. There, tucked into the pages of my diary, is the green receipt from the dry cleaning concession in the tube station precinct. The receipt for the suit I should have collected on the way home from work last night. I carry on reading. *Lunch will be ham and salad on granary bread, mayonnaise but no butter, and a bottle of orange juice. You will also buy a banana, the greenest and most unripe in the sandwich bar. You will not eat the banana. Instead, you will use it to pleasure yourself at your desk, and you will think of me while you do so.*

I read the last couple of sentences again. This is something new. Something dangerous. It wouldn't be the first time I've played with myself at work. In the early days of our relationship, before I had ever begun to explore the submissive side of my personality, Michael used to send me emails describing what he was going to do to me when I got home, emails so filthy and explicit I would rush off to the ladies' and bring myself to a swift, sharp climax, muffling my moans by jamming the fleshy part of my thumb into my mouth. But in the relative open of my office, where someone could walk in and catch me at it? Of course, I could go home and just tell Michael I'd done as he instructed. But he would know. He always knows when I try to disobey him, however careful or sneaky I try to be. And besides, the thought excites me just as much as it alarms me. It must do: otherwise why would my pussy be pulsing quite so hard against the silky crotch of my underwear?

Time drags for the next hour. It's almost impossible to concentrate on my work; all I can think of are Michael's instructions, but then I'm sure he intended it that way. Finally, it's one o'clock, and I log off my workstation, grab my handbag and go out to get my lunch.

It's unseasonably warm, and people have left their coats and jackets indoors and are basking in the spring sunshine. As I wait to cross the road, I find myself, as always, watching the women who pass by, checking them out to see if they bear some subtle mark of ownership. I can spot the signs by now: the discreet tattoo on the ankle or shoulder blade; the black velvet choker or thick silver band around the neck that is rather more than just a fashionable piece of jewelry.

There are scenes being played out all around us every day, as seemingly mundane yet undeniably kinky as the one between Michael and me. Sometimes, you can walk into one without even realizing it. We were shopping in town the other week, and he came in the changing rooms with me as I went to try on a dress. As we made our way down the row of cubicles to find one that was vacant, a curtain was suddenly whisked aside by the man who stood outside it. He made some casual enquiry to his wife about the bathing suit she was squeezing into, as though he hadn't noticed we were there, and all the time he was giving us a perfect view of her body, tits and pussy blatantly on display and the sky blue fabric of the swimsuit bunched around her knees. Her face was blushing red, and yet I saw in her eyes the thrill she was getting from her exposure and humiliation. This was what got the two of them off, and I was sure that when Michael and I had gone, he would pin her up against the cubicle partition and fuck her to a standstill as they teased each other about what they had just done.

It worked for them, just as my lunchtime ritual works for me, this setting of a so-simple rule that marks the level of trust between Michael and me.

For once there's no queue in the sandwich bar, and I give my order to the young man behind the counter, one of the extended family of Turks who own the place. He's chatty as always, but I'm not listening to a word he's saying, just nodding when he holds up the pepper mill, muttering a token word of thanks as he hands the sandwich, wrapped in a paper bag, to me. All I'm thinking about is the fruit bowl next to the till, and the slender, underripe banana I reach out and take from it. As I hand over my money to the girl behind the till, I think I see her glance at the banana and smile. Does she realize what I'm going to do with it? Is it really as obvious to everyone as I feel it must be? My cheeks flush scarlet, and then she says something in Turkish and I realize she's responding to some conversation in the kitchen, nothing to do with me at all. Chastened, I pocket my change without checking it and make my way back to the office on autopilot, the last ordinary act of this extraordinary lunch hour.

I don't even unwrap the sandwich; I have no appetite for food, just a nervous fluttering in my stomach and an answering pulse between my legs. The door to my office doesn't lock, so I jam the wastepaper basket up against it. Anyone tries to come in and I'll hear the rattle and stop what I'm doing—assuming I'm not too far gone to stop, that is.

Quickly, inelegantly, I reach up under my skirt and yank down my knickers. I haven't even touched myself yet and they are already sticky with my juice. Michael's orders and my own imagination have got me this excited, and I only wish he was here to watch me.

Making myself as comfortable as I can in my chair, I push my skirt up and spread my legs. I can feel the fabric of the seat cover, rough and prickly against my bare arse. I'm trying to remember every sensation, every detail, because I suspect that when I get home, I will be asked to describe it to my husband, reliving every deliciously dirty moment of what I'm about to do.

The banana is firm in my hand, and feels cool to the touch as I run the blunt head along the length of my sex. If Michael were here, he would want me to take my time, make sure I'm wet and open enough to take this unorthodox toy, just as he likes it when I spend long, lazy moments fingering my clit and gently teasing my hole, getting it ready for my favorite dildo or the hot length of his cock. But time is the one thing I don't have, not when the boys in the advertising department could be back, loud and boisterous, from their liquid lunch at any moment. If this was a fantasy that I was spinning for Michael, of course, they would blunder in and catch me, force me to continue as I tried to cover myself up, make me bare my tits for them, maybe even queue up to fuck me in turn over the desk, ramming their cocks into my pussy as the flesh of the banana oozed out around their thrusts. But this is real life—however skewed—and all I have are my own busily working fingers to stroke me and stretch me open.

It doesn't take long before I know I'm ready to be filled. Eyes closed, breathing hard, I press the banana home, feeling the strange, hard ridges sliding against my soft flesh. I know this is the most perverse, most risky, most potentially career-threatening thing I have ever done. And yet I do it gladly. I do it because Michael asks it of me, and when he asks, I answer with my obedience. I do it to show my submission to this man I love so very much.

My feet are up on the desk now, the wheels of my chair squeaking rhythmically on the floor as I fuck myself with a piece of fruit. There could be a whole crowd watching me at play, and I wouldn't know. And if I knew, I wouldn't care. As he wanted, as he instructed, I am thinking of him—and only him—as the steady thrusting of the banana and the delicate pressure of my finger on my clit pushes me over the edge.

When my head clears and my knees are steady enough that I can stand up without trembling, I wrap the ruined banana in one of the napkins that came with my sandwich. It will still be there at the end of the day, just as the receipt for Michael's suit will still be in my drawer. I really should remember to collect that dry cleaning, but I'm prepared to suffer the consequences. After all, who knows what I might be having for lunch tomorrow?

SCHOOLGIRL AND ANGEL

Thomas S. Roche

S he stood there at the very edge of my swing space, watching with evident rapture and squirming her ass back and forth in her tight little schoolgirl's skirt. This section of the dungeon was brighter than the rest, because it's where the heavy punishment took place. Therefore, it was easy for me to see her in the long line of mirrors behind the St. Andrew's cross.

I've always bitched about those mirrors at The Sanctuary—an accident with a singletail could shatter one of them in an instant—but at the moment, I was happy they were there, if only because she looked so good in the skirt. The fact that she wasn't wearing anything but a skimpy white bra on top added to the pleasure of it. Her tits were magnificent, and the mesh bra was mostly see-through. Her nipples stood pink and erect through the thin fabric.

Her hair was black, obviously dyed. I could tell from the cut of her pretty face that she was well into the time of life when that hair was probably gray under its artificial coloring. She had the look of the early-forty-something latecomer to the dungeon—eyes wide and fascination obvious with everything she saw. I had watched her sauntering around the dungeon, turning down come-ons from an endless line of leather-clad Daddy types; despite this, her arousal was evident.

Perhaps a half hour ago she had brushed by me in the crowded dungeon, and the scent of her had been enough to make my cock hard in my blue jeans.

Angel was squirming, too, not least because of the hot line of stripes I was placing across her beautiful ass with my newest flogger. After a warm-up with my hands and the lightest flogger I had, she had counted to twelve, obediently, each time saying, "Thank you, Sir, may I have another?" which was her own particular turn-on, not mine.

She was reaching her limit, though. The reddening of her ass didn't tell me that, but the tug of her body against the chains of the St. Andrew's cross did.

"Just a little punishment," she'd told me, and I'd pursed my lips trying to hide my disappointment. With Angel, delicious as she is, "a little punishment" means half a spank and a minimal tweak of the nipples. Then, without fail, she was ready to fuck.

Now, as I laid on strokes thirteen, fourteen, and fifteen, she began to add "Ow!" and "Eeech!" sounds to every "Thank you, Sir," and I felt the pulse in my muscles that made me want to lay it on thicker—and the torture in my nice-guy soul that made me hold back.

Now, the older woman was creeping closer, leaning in to the bubble of play, invading my swing space in a way that I could hardly hold against her, since I kept inching back.

"Care to take a swing?" I asked her, turning and holding out the butt of the flogger. Angel and I had a curious kind of agreement—when she's tied up, anyone I wish can hit her, provided they don't hit her too hard.

The older woman gave the most girlish of giggles, hiding her pinkening face behind her hand. Her green eyes danced.

"Oh, God no," she said, her flirting obvious. "I could never hit another woman."

I smiled. "It's fun," I said.

Her eyes brightened slightly, a wicked smile playing across her red-painted lips.

"I'm sure she's having more fun than you are."

Angel had started to squirm some more, so I gave her three more blows in rapid succession without giving her a chance to thank me. She said "Ow! Ow! Ow!" emphatically rather than doing so, and I felt a rush of top's guilt.

I came up behind Angel, put my hand tenderly on her ass, feeling it squirm under my fingers.

"Too much?"

She shrugged, an odd gesture when one is strapped to a St. Andrew's cross. "Maybe I'm just not in the mood for a flogging. You mind?"

"Not at all," I said, reaching for the restraints. "Need a cool down?"

"Nah, I'm good," she said with a casualness that made it seem like I had asked if she wanted another beer.

"I'll let you down, then." I kissed Angel on the side of the neck.

"What's with Demi Moore?" whispered Angel when my face came close.

It took me a minute to figure out what she was talking about. There was no resemblance, really, but the woman in the schoolgirl outfit did have the sultry look of the over-forty sexpot. Angel is always making snarky comments about the older women in the scene—and since she's the same age as me, twenty-three, to her that's pretty much all of them.

I shrugged. Lips close to Angel's ear, I said, "I don't know. She's watching."

"So, ask her to play!" hissed Angel. "She's obviously into you!"

I glanced back at the schoolgirl, who was staring at us with big, wide eyes.

"I think she's into *you*," I said bitterly. With her bleached, close-cropped hair and pierced nipples, Angel's the one who invariably draws the ladies.

"Bullshit," Angel whispered. "She's *such* a bottom." I finished with Angel's wrists and bent down to unfasten her ankle restraints. When I came back up she turned, kissed me, and growled, "I'm going to have one of those apple fritters, and when I come back if she's not at the very least strapped to this fucking thing, if not polishing your knob, I'm going to be very unhappy."

I cocked my head down at her. "You serious?"

Angel looked over at the schoolgirl and smiled. The schoolgirl simply smiled back.

"Oh yeah," Angel said. "If ever a look said 'fuck me bow-legged,' that's the look. Just know I'll be watching. After the fritter."

Angel bent down and retrieved her thong from the base of the cross. She stepped into it, then walked away, glancing over her shoulder to wink at me.

Angel and I had drawn a small crowd, pressing close in a sea of leather and flesh. The schoolgirl was closest, the only one to break the bubble and be slightly inside the line of blue tape on the cheap industrial carpet.

I held up the flogger and gestured at the cross. "Ladies? Gentlemen? We have a free cross. Anyone? Anyone?"

No one stepped up or made a sound, except for a faint rustling as the spectators seemed to shrink back slightly.

All except the schoolgirl.

I have never been good with picking up strange women at play parties. In fact, if Angel wasn't a particularly aggressive woman, I probably would never get anywhere. But now, my heart pounding, I managed to make an inviting gesture to the schoolgirl. I raised my eyebrows at her; she only stared with those fiery green eyes.

"Whips? Chains? Carefully calculated agony? Sexual degradation before a slavering crowd?"

The schoolgirl giggled.

"Is that your pick-up line?"

"I'm afraid it's the best I can do," I said. "I'm not much of a flirt."

Her gaze slid like butter over my legs, my cock, my face, and then came down to rest hungrily on the flogger in my hand.

"Can you hit any harder than you hit her?"

I put my hand over my heart.

"It wounds me that you'd need to ask!"

"Mmmm," she said, moving toward the cross. "Then I'm game. I like it on the pussy, though—mind if I'm facing out?"

"Uh," I said. "S-sure. Uh...how hard?"

She giggled, covering her mouth with her hands in that coquettish gesture that made my cock shudder. Her eyes had lowered to the bulge in my jeans.

"As hard as that?" she asked, and we both knew what we meant.

"Not even close," I said. "But I can try. What's your name?" I asked.

"Oh, just call me Schoolgirl," she said. "Please tell me *your* name isn't 'Darkness Master' or 'Lord of Shadows.'"

I pursed my lips, feigning annoyance.

"It's Daddy," I said. "That is, if Schoolgirl's *your* real name."

"It most certainly is," she said, looking as offended as a woman in chains can look.

"Your real father must have been a real pervert, then."

"Yes, Daddy," she sighed.

She smoothly stepped out of the skirt. She folded it neatly and doffed her bra with the calculated elegance of a woman who knows her breasts are absolutely beyond glorious. They were, full and firm and capped by those nipples I'd been watching through the bra.

Underneath she had a white garter belt and stockings, which I'd already known, given that there wasn't much to that skirt. What I didn't know was that she'd been savvy enough to wear her lacy white panties on the outside of her garters, so it came away easily as she took off her skirt. She smiled at me and tossed me her underwear. I caught it in one hand and resisted the urge to bring it to my face; I didn't need to, because I could smell her on it, wet and sharp and horny.

She leaned back against the cross, legs spread, smiling at me as I draped her panties on a stray eyebolt on the edge of the cross.

As I looked her over, she spread her legs a little wider and got more comfortable on the cross. The posture suited her immensely well.

"Ready when you are, Daddy," she said.

Her pussy was shaved, the tattoo of a coiled snake striking downward to bite her clit.

I hadn't expected my ham-handed come-on to work. Angel, more turned on by imagining my potential exploits than I am, is always trying to push me at available-looking women. It never,

ever works—probably because my response is usually to turn red and hide behind her.

There was no Angel to hide behind now, and Schoolgirl wasn't leaving much to the imagination.

"All right, Daddy," she cooed. "Tie me up."

I was frozen for a minute, looking over that glorious body. I came toward her, reaching for the restraints.

This cross was leaned back at an inviting angle, requiring me to lean against her a little as I secured her wrists. Her breasts were against me, her nipples so hard I could feel them against my chest through the thin T-shirt I wore. I could also feel my cock pressing hard through my jeans, against her smooth belly. She squirmed a little against me, making my cock ache. I could smell her: the scent of a horny female body with a hint of shampoo, soap, something sufficiently feminine to remind me, in case there was any chance I'd forgotten, that this was a breathtakingly sexy woman I was strapping naked to a cross.

"You know, snakes don't strike downward," I said nervously, providing a fact that I'd completely made up.

"I hope *you* do," she said with a smile, her breath sweet in my face as I circled her wrist in the padded leather.

"Should we do all that safeword crap?"

"I've watched you," she said, and I felt my face flushing. "You can tell. Besides, 'safeword' works if it really gets down to it."

"You just want a flogging? On, er, on your pussy?"

I was leaning close enough that she could do it without much effort, the movement of her face to mine sure and confident. She planted her lips on mine and I tasted her tongue, felt the post through it grazing my lips.

"Oh, I want *so* much more than a flogging on my pussy, Daddy," she sighed when our lips came apart, a delicate filament of spit crackling between them. "But there's your pretty little girlfriend to consider."

I secured Schoolgirl's other wrist and shrugged. "She likes to share."

Schoolgirl giggled, this time unable to hide her mouth behind her hand.

"Then skip the flogging for now," she said with a wicked look.

I knelt down between her legs, the scent of her pussy sending a pulse through me as I secured first one ankle, then the other. I glanced up at her and had to fight the urge to press my mouth to her cunt, take a big hungry bite where the snake was striking. Her lips were slim and slight, but her clit was enormous, begging for attention. Erect, it almost reminded me of a crooked finger, summoning me in.

Her eyes were doing the same. I don't know if she nodded or I merely read the hunger there. But I was so fucking hard I wasn't thinking straight, and a top—*especially* a Daddy—must always, always think straight. Mustn't he?

My mouth descended between her legs hungrily, and I found her clit with my tongue. She let out a sudden, ecstatic moan of pleasure, and my pounding heart gave a flutter as she ground her body against mine, coaxing me deeper into her sex.

She was so wet that the flick of my tongue between her small, tight lips brought a bead of moisture leaking out and onto my chin. I licked deeper and she shuddered against the cross, pulling violently on her restraints as if completely out of control of her actions.

I drew back and looked up at her, feeling stupid for wondering if this was consent—a moan and a squirm and a shiver.

She met my gaze and said in a musical voice rich with sarcasm, loud enough for the spectators to hear: "Oh, no, Daddy. Not there. Don't lick me *there*—it's too dirty. Filthy, dirty,

Daddy—anything but that, *please,* Daddy!"

A vicious kind of arousal coursed through me, then, the kind that makes my stomach twirl and my heart beat like a jackhammer. And my cock got so hard that, as they say, it didn't have a conscience, even a conscience of the sex-positive, socially responsible kind.

I had never had any woman talk to me like that—not even Angel, after all-night discussions about how the hottest thing she could do was surprise me with how perverse she was. She was perverse, don't get me wrong—but she was not the verbal type.

I had the creepy feeling of being watched, and not only by the multitudes of strangers who had crowded around to see Schoolgirl on the cross. When I glanced over my shoulder, there was Angel, apple fritter in one hand, her other hand making an enthusiastic thumbs-up sign as she gave me a stage wink that would have done Eric Idle proud. Her tongue made an obscene thrust into the ripped-open guts of the custard-filled fritter, the slurp audible even across the play floor. Angel could be such a frat boy sometimes.

I looked up again and Schoolgirl looked down at me with hunger in her eyes, her mouth hanging slack in silent encouragement/enticement/approval. I brought my mouth to her cunt and hungrily began to work my tongue against her, savoring the cries she gave as I drew circles around her clit, suckled on it, caressed her inner thighs.

Her cunt held such inexplicable magnetism that I was a little surprised when I found my two fingers sliding easily into its tight embrace—and even more surprised when I heard Schoolgirl crying out and felt her grinding herself onto my hand, pushing my fingers deeper.

Her G-spot was swollen, full. I could feel its spongy curve against my fingertips and feel her whole body tense and shiver when I pressed firmly against it. I continued to tongue her clit, finger fucking her rhythmically in a come-hither gesture of my own, while my cock pulsed with every stroke.

"Fuck, Daddy," she gasped. "Where did you learn to do that?"

I took my mouth off her sex long enough to say, "Same place you learned to pick up strangers and call them Daddy—in the gutter."

I almost thought I saw her blush, but that didn't lessen her enthusiasm as I went back to licking her. Her juices dripped wetly down my hand and onto my arm, and her cries rose in pitch, her legs tensing.

She was going to come.

I'm not sure what made me stop—if, as a top, as a *Daddy,* I wasn't ready for my victim—my little girl—to come—or if the sudden power of my tongue and my fingers terrified me, this stranger's response was too right, too perfect, for me to accept it into my brain.

I stood up, slipping my fingers out of her—I think I had it in my brain to ask her if she was all right, if this was all right, if it was okay to finger her and lick her clit and make her come. Which might seem stupid in retrospect, but this had all happened so fast I still didn't quite believe it was real.

A glance over my shoulder told me it wasn't Angel stopping me—on the contrary, she'd managed to drag over a nearby folding chair and was propped on it, legs spread, eyes wide, one hand pinching her own nipple, the other hand down her thong.

So I turned back to Schoolgirl, and leaned close to whisper something—anything—anything to break the tension, the overwhelming sense that if I didn't fuck her silly right then, right there.

When I came in close to her face she caught my mouth and kissed it, tongue sliding deep, as if hungry for my mouth, for her own juices. She ground her body against mine, her nipples rubbing firm, her body shaking against the chains.

"Can you fuck standing up?" she whispered, performing a deft motion to bring one thigh into contact with my cock.

"You asked me for a flogging," I said.

Then a delicate shiver went through her naked body, and the look in her eyes was enough to make me fuck her right there, against the slanted cross, with a roomful of perverts watching. If only it hadn't been for what she said next.

"Oh, no, Daddy," she said, voice shaking. "Not a flogging. Don't whip my thighs, Daddy, please—not my pussy, Daddy, please, *please* don't whip my pussy, anything but that!" Her voice was thick with desire.

My hand was already on my flogger. I stepped back, cock throbbing, eyes fixed on the cunt that still glistened with my spittle. I drew the flogger around in a big, easy circle, wishing I had a smaller one to start with—but not really caring.

The first blow struck her exposed cunt with a swish and a slap and another swish. It brought a thunderous moan from Schoolgirl's lips, and an echo-like "Oh, yeah," from behind me—Angel. She always did like watching other women get punished; she's not much of a masochist herself.

When I looked back, her hand was deeper in her thong than it had been before—and her eyes were on me, not my victim.

I brought the flogger around again, striking her cunt harder this time. She moaned louder, threw her head back, and groaned on the verge of a scream, and I hesitated with the next blow until I saw her head lowering, eyes meeting mine, and heard her moan, "Green, Daddy."

I hit her again, and she squirmed and trembled on the cross, gasping, whimpering. Again, and she all but went slack in her bonds, leaning hard against the cross. This time, she didn't say,

"Green," but rather, "Fuck me. Fuck me, Daddy."

I had that sudden sense of a person in my swing space, but by the time I looked around, Angel's hands were already around me from behind, her hands deftly working my belt. She had a condom tucked between her fingers, the wrapper already discarded. She got my cock out and stroked it slowly up and down, pinching the condom's head and smoothly rolling it down.

"If you don't fuck that schoolgirl right now," Angel growled, "I'll never forgive you. And neither will she."

Schoolgirl stretched on the cross, moaning, lifting her ass toward me, grinding her hips rhythmically. I dropped the flogger then, and lunged toward her, hearing her softly whimpered "Fuck me, Daddy," all but silenced by my mouth on hers.

My cockhead slipped easily between those small lips. She was even wetter than when I'd left her. My first thrust brought a deafening groan from her lips, her body so tight around my cock that I would have come immediately if not for the condom. I leaned heavily against her as I began to fuck her. My fingers pinched her nipples, softly at first and then harder as she choked out, "Yes, Daddy," and each thrust brought a louder moan—until she came, her muscles clenching my shaft, her body straining against the chains as she strove to fuck herself onto me, to meet every thrust with one of her own. As she came, she screamed my name, "Daddy!" so loud she all but deafened me.

But there weren't many more thrusts—because I was so fucking turned on that I came a moment later, grasping her long black hair and tangling it in my fist as I held my schoolgirl in place to kiss her, hard and deep, still tasting her cunt. When the strength went out of my thighs, she caught me neatly between hers, holding me up as I slumped against the cross and against her.

"Need a hand?" came a whisper from Angel as she reached

down between Schoolgirl's thighs and helped secure the condom while my cock slipped out of her.

"Did you train him?" sighed Schoolgirl as Angel leaned close.

Angel cocked her head at Schoolgirl.

"I mean...that's quite a tongue he's got. And quite a cock. Did you..."

Angel gave me that sarcastic look she's famous for. She shrugged.

"I'm sure nobody could ever train *him*," she said.

Schoolgirl's lips, all smeared red lipstick and the faintest hint of a smile, gave her own shrug, rattling the chains.

"I'm not so sure," said Schoolgirl. "Maybe it just takes two."

"Maybe," said Angel suspiciously, and, without asking, leaned in to kiss Schoolgirl, who not only didn't argue but moaned softly as their tongues met.

We got Schoolgirl down from the cross and took her home with us so fast we forgot her panties.

As it turned out, though, she didn't need them.

FIRST DATE
WITH THE DOM

Noelle Keely

A hot summer day in Boston had morphed into a sultry night by the time Serena and Jack dragged themselves out of the Barking Crab. Still talking, they made their way across Fort Point Channel to South Station, where Serena would need to catch the T if she was heading home to Dorchester.

Then came the inevitable moment where they stood on the street and stared at each other, trying to figure out what to do next.

What they both wanted was obvious.

Serena could smell it over the combination of salt and exhaust fumes that scented the air this close to the harbor. She could taste it, as she could still taste Jack's fingers. She could feel it in her blood and bones as much as in her tight, sensitive nipples and wet, pulsing pussy.

Desire. Need. Want.

Hunger.

All the dark creatures that lived inside her brain clamored

for their chance to come out to play: the broken virgin, the whore, the temple dancer, the pirate's captive, the French maid, the prisoner of the Inquisition.

And the slave, always the slave.

But she didn't dare to speak.

Odd, that. In the past, when she'd wanted a man anywhere as badly as she wanted Jack, she hadn't waited around for him to make a move. Oh, no, she'd made her dishonorable intentions clear.

But Jack froze that bold part of her, even while he melted the rest. Jack's pale, steady gaze and cool voice and the knowledge of what he was and the feeling that he wouldn't react well to being pushed, held her back.

So Serena bit her lip and waited.

For what must have only been about thirty seconds, but felt more like thirty minutes.

The hell with being decorous, she decided. If she was stepping out of line, he'd let her know. And with any luck, the way he let her know might be fun.

She stretched up, put her arms around Jack's neck and kissed him.

He didn't seem to mind, judging from the way he pulled her closer, the way he met her tongue with his and orchestrated their dance.

But he pulled away after a distressingly short time and looked down at her rather sternly. "Patience, pretty lady," he said, shaking his head. "I prefer to set the pace."

For a second, she thought she might have actually angered him. He seemed remote and somehow bigger: taller, broader, more menacing, almost frightening.

It was a type of frightening, though, that went straight to her groin, stabbing at her clit.

Then one of his hands buried itself in the thick curls at the back of her neck and pulled her head back. "Fortunately," he whispered, "you were only about two seconds ahead of me."

He kissed her.

Such simple words: she could tell her mother the next time they talked, "And then Jack kissed me," and her mother would say something along the lines of "How sweet!"

Sweet, though, had nothing to do with this devouring, possessive mouth, this fierce grip on her hair, this other hand firmly cupping her ass and pressing her pelvis against his body. Sweet had nothing to do with the conflagration roaring through her body, burning up her will to do anything for the moment but touch Jack, please Jack, be pleased by Jack. And "sweet" certainly had nothing to do with the hard cock pushing against her as if it could penetrate her through their clothes, there on the corner of Atlantic Avenue by South Station.

If it could, she'd let him.

As it was, she was going to take what she could get, here on the street. As long as he didn't mind, that is.

She moved experimentally against him, shifting so her clit, through the thin fabric of her dress and panties, was in contact with him. Then, thinking fast, she broke from the kiss just long enough to ask, "Is this all right?"

"Oh, yes," he whispered, his breath hot against her ear. "That's a good girl. See if you can make yourself come by rubbing yourself against me. I'll reward you if you can."

Oh, my god. If she'd been turned on before, she was about a hundred times more so now just by hearing him say these words.

It was early enough that the streets were still full, pedestrians stepping around the island they made in the sea of foot traffic, sometimes with an indulgent laugh, sometimes not. Some little piece of brain still grounded in the everyday world said she should be self-conscious, ashamed of such slutty behavior in public.

Serena told that little piece of brain to shut the hell up.

Serena ground against Jack, thrusting her pelvis wantonly against the bulge in his pants as they kissed.

Each movement sent little fingers of pleasure through her, reaching up to meet the pleasure flowing down from the lips Jack was still devouring. It was enough to feel amazing, but not enough to push her over the edge. She shifted, meaning to straddle his thigh—it was subtle as a ton of bricks falling on your head, but maybe any gawking passersby would be having extrahot evenings themselves—but Jack put both hands on her hips and moved her back where she had been.

"Oh, no, I'm not making it that easy," he chuckled. "Besides, I like you rubbing your pussy against my cock right here on the street." He nibbled her neck then returned his lips to her ear. "A bus just went past, and everyone on it saw you getting yourself off. All the pedestrians, all the drivers...they're all looking at you, thinking you're a hot little slut."

"And that we're both drunk, because adults just don't act like this when they're sober."

His voice was pushing her. He still had her hips in his grasp and was moving her, getting her to push and grind in particular ways that must have been good for him, but were also doing crazy things to her. "They'll never know," he said, his voice gravelly with desire, "that you're doing this because I told you to. But you'll know, won't you?"

Each word felt like a lick on her clit. Her body began to tremble uncontrollably, and she pressed her face against his chest, trying not to scream.

"You're going to come for me right now." It wasn't a question.

The trembling turned to violent shakes. Her pussy spasmed, and she wished Jack was inside her. The street around her vanished, lost in a flood of sensation.

And despite herself, Serena did scream, muffled against Jack's broad chest.

He shifted so his arms were around her, possessively but far more gently than they had been, and he cuddled her close, nuzzling at her hair. "Good girl," he said. "That's my good girl." The pride and desire in his voice danced across Serena's skin and caused little aftershocks in her dripping pussy.

And he just held her that way until she stopped trembling, as seemingly oblivious to other people during this tender moment as he had been during the lewd one.

After that, the only real question was whose place they would go to, and that one was simple. Serena had a roommate, Jack didn't. And so they headed to where Jack had left his car.

On a quiet side street in the financial district, Jack stopped her. "Take off your panties," he ordered abruptly.

"Wha...?" Serena hoped she didn't look as foolish as she sounded.

"I bet they're soaked through. Aren't they?"

She nodded mutely. They had been at least since he'd fed her the squid, but articulating that was too much for her brain at the moment.

"Already sticky enough out tonight without sticky panties, too. So lose them."

She looked around. The street was deserted except for a couple of men having a smoke outside the restaurant on the corner. They were apparently having a heated conversation, unlikely to pay attention to something happening up the block. Still, it seemed a little public. Being pantyless wasn't the problem; no one would ever know for sure under her full-skirted sundress unless she tripped or had some other accident so spectacular that lack of underwear would be the least of her worries. It was getting them off gracefully.

She hesitated, half of her screaming to obey Jack and see what further adventures it led to, the other half too embarrassed to move.

"Problem?" he asked, in a tone she couldn't read.

Serena nodded, then shook her head. Why was this so hard? She'd slithered out of wet bikini bottoms under a skirt before; it was the same principle.

"We haven't talked about limits yet, or set any ground rules. You can say no. I'd just want to know why if you do, if it's a hard limit or just something you're not ready for tonight."

And knowing that she could say no somehow made it easier to say yes, and to work the panties down while leaning on him for balance.

By the time she bent down to retrieve them from around her ankle, she could feel her juices on the top of her thighs.

Before she could shove them into her bag, Jack embraced her, gently enough, but effectively pinioning her arms to her sides.

The panties hung limp in her hand—the hand that was facing the street, for anyone to see.

Despite an overwhelming urge to crunch the tiny thong into her fist, she didn't move. Part of her brain that she wouldn't have thought could function under these conditions recognized the test and saw the right, desired—desirable—answer in the same blinding flash.

Jack liked teasing. Jack liked testing. Jack wanted to know what she wanted, what she didn't want, what her limits were; but they hadn't had a chance to talk about it yet. And by letting her know she could say no, he'd forced her to think about whether her urge to curl up and die was merely a knee-jerk reaction.

It was.

All this flashed through her brain in a millisecond. Then he kissed her and all efforts at thinking pretty much stopped.

There was laughter and the sound of footsteps.

She opened her eyes, peered around Jack as best she could.

A small group of older women was approaching, all wearing logo caps from a popular tourist pub and giggling as if they'd spent the early evening sampling the pub's wares. Gray-haired and solid looking, dressed in clothes that owed more to comfort than fashion, they reminded her of her mom.

Panic flared.

And then faded. Funny, but with Jack's arms around her, she felt safe to do things she'd only fantasized about before. Not that she'd especially fantasized about showing a bunch of motherly strangers what a tart she was, but "forced" exhibitionism had definitely been in her top ten masturbatory hits.

"You're thinking too much again," Jack murmured, and resumed the kiss.

As the tipsy tourists passed them, she overheard a shocked—or maybe amused—exclamation of "Now that's not something you see every day!" and a lot more laughter.

Serena trembled and clenched, so excited by the situation and the fact of being caught that she was almost ready to come again without being touched.

"Time to get you home, my girl," Jack whispered in her ear.

And those words, that possessive tone was all it took to bring her off again, coming on the streets of the financial district for the second time that night.

IN CONTROL

M. Christian

We met in the dark corner of an Internet chatroom. SLUT-SLAVE, a nubile profile full of in-the-know vernacular with damned good typing skills, and MASTER017, my digital persona. We didn't really meet there, of course, but that's where we first started to talk. The dance was slow, at first. I've heard other doms say that they don't like it slow, sedate, careful—they'd rather snap their fingers and have them drop to their knees. Me? I like the dance, the approach, the "chat" in chatroom. Besides, I've had a few of my own snaps, the eager young slaves with sparkles in their eyes and not a clue between the ears. Give me someone who knows what they're getting into. It's better, after all, to be wanted by someone who wants the best, as opposed to someone who just wants.

So we danced, we chatted, SLUTSLAVE and I—or at least that cyberspace mask I wore. Finally, after many a midnight typing, she complained with a sideways smile [;-)] that she was looking for something where more than her wrists got a workout.

Like I said: step one, two, three, turn, step one, two, three. Careful moves in this courtship dance. No snap from me. I made her sing for her supper, pushing her along, not making it easy for her. "Do you know what you're asking for, slave?" I asked, clicking and clacking on my keyboard.

She did the same, and the dance changed its tempo: "Yes, Master. I do."

We made a date to get together the next weekend.

A knock on the door. Normally, even when it's expected, it can be jarring. Fist on wood. Bang, bang, bang! But not that night. I opened it. "Welcome."

I had a picture, of course, and the flesh was just like it, though filled out in three-dimensional reality. Unlike the door, seeing her jarred me, but not unpleasantly.

"Thanks," she said with a smile, walking in. I closed the door behind her. Full bodied, curved, somewhere between too young and too old, tight and firm from exercise. Eyes gleaming with sharpness, mouth parted just so with anticipation. Curly dark hair, her skin a Mediterranean patina.

We didn't have to say much, most of our negotiations having been done in emails back and forth. I knew she couldn't stay on her feet for too long (plantar fasciitis), and didn't like metal re-straints or canes—all of it. But her list of yeses was longer than her list of nos.

"Stand there," I said, pointing to the center of my wool rug. My room looked odd, with all the furniture pushed back, piled up: spare chairs on my big oak table, ottoman tucked under-neath. The room was only the rug, a coarse wool bull's-eye, and my favorite plush wingback.

"Yes, sir," she said, the grin never leaving her lips, as she walked to the center.

"Stop." She did, turning slowly to face me. Her breasts were big, wide. Not a girl's, a woman's. Twin peaks on cotton fabric. No bra, as ordered. I reached out to one of the points, circled it slowly with a stiff finger. The smile stayed, but her breathing deepened, sped up. "Did I tell you what to call me?"

"No—" she hissed, trying to swallow a scream, as I pinched her nipple, hard. One of my nos concerned sound. My apartment had thin walls.

"Call me 'Master,'" I said, low and mean, grumbling and growling, as I pinched even more.

"Yes ... M-Master," she said, with a delightful stammer against the pain.

I released the pressure. "Pain is your punishment. It will be frequent. Pleasure is your reward. It will be rare. I'm not going to ask you if you understand. If you didn't you wouldn't be here. Undress."

She did, sensually but efficiently. The white cotton dress went first. Under was a pair of everyday panties, just white. No hose, only socks and shoes, as I had requested. Lingerie doesn't interest me. Bodies don't even interest me. She didn't interest me. But what I could do to her—that was what interested me.

She was naked. Her body was good. Not ideal, but with a warmth and reality to her. Big, full tits with just enough sag to mean reality and not silicone or somesuch. A plump little tummy. A plump mons with a gentle tuft of dark hair. It wasn't a body that you'd hang on your wall, but it was a body you'd want to fuck. But that was on her no list, which was fine by me. I definitely wanted to fuck with her, not just with her body.

Her hands kept drifting up, a force of will keeping them from hiding her breasts, covering her nipples. I smiled. SLUT-SLAVE had a modest streak. Priceless.

I got out my toolbag, my own kind of wry smile on my face.

Other tops went on and on about their toys, pissing on each other about the quality of the leather, the weight, the evilness of certain objects. I sat back and watched them: wry grin then, wry grin now. If I had a headboard, I'd have it carved: *A workman is as good as his tools,* it would say. *A great one doesn't need them at all.*

I added it up once. Fifty dollars was as high as I got. Show me any other hobby that could give as much pleasure as my little bag of toys—or as much wonderful discomfort to SLUTSLAVE.

I laid them out on the rug in front of her. I felt like a surgeon—or a priest. "We're going to play a game," I said. "The rules are very simple. I ask a question. If you tell me the truth, you get a reward. If you don't, you get punished. Again, I won't ask if you understand."

I picked up a favorite—though, to tell my own truth, I like them all. This one was the favorite of the moment. I squeezed, and the clothespin yawned open. I held it out to her nipple, which, I noticed, was nicely wrinkled, and erect. "Are you wet?"

"Yes," she said in a breathy whisper. I could tell before she answered; her musk was thick in the room. I was hard. Hell, I was hard when I opened the front door, but hearing that, knowing that, my jeans grew that much tighter.

"First lesson. It's an important one. Sometimes even the truth can mean pain," I said, in my best of voices, as I released the spring on the clothespin, letting it bite down sharp and quick on her thickening nipple.

Her sigh was a lovely musical tone, a bass rumble of pain that peaked toward pleasure. Oh, yes, that was it. The first note of a long musical composition. Her knees buckled because of it, and I put a hand on her shoulder to steady her.

I kept it on for a mental beat of ten. Not long, but long enough. I released it, keeping my hand on her shoulder. It always hurts so much worse coming off than it does coming on. Sure enough, her knees buckled even more and she slipped, dropped down to my rug.

Still on her knees, breathing much more regularly, she looked up at me, chin level with my crotch. I knew if I said to, she'd unzip my fly, undo my belt, reach in with eager, strong fingers to fish out my dick, stick it into her hot mouth. She'd do it, I knew, but like the clothespin, it's so much better if you wait. So I did.

I stepped back, grinning at the flicker of disappointment on her face. You'll have to wait too, I thought. I retrieved my bag, and sat down in my chair, facing her. The clothespin was still in my hand and I found myself absently opening and closing it. A dom's worry bead, I guess. "Stand up. Right now."

She did. Her knees seemed a bit weak. "Come closer." She did, her gait slow and controlled. I reached down to my bag at my feet and picked up something new. "You're mine. You belong to me," I said, looking into her face. Her eyes shone. "I won't ask if you understand."

When I was a kid, I used to play with dolls. Well, maybe not "dolls," not exactly. No Raggedy Anns, no Barbies—not like that. I liked that they were mine, they belonged to me. I could make them do anything, at any time, and they didn't say a word. They just did it, forever smiling.

It was a new toy, another deceivingly simple thing. I saw it in some import/export place down in the city. Elegant and simple, black and glossy. Seeing it, I knew I had to have it. Having it, I couldn't wait to use it.

"Lean back," I said. I was tapping it against my palm, a lacquered metronome. Tilted back, her breasts swayed gently apart, only beginning to make that armpit migration—she was younger than I thought.

I ran the tip of the chopstick around her right nipple, feeling it skip and slide over her areola, the contours traveling down the length of it into my fingertips. She signed, softly.

Way back when, right after I outgrew those plastic dolls, I wondered if I had a dead thing—you know, preferring girls stiff and cold rather than warm and breathing. But that wasn't it. It wasn't their being immobile, plastic, it was my being in control, making them do what I wanted. Right then, she was my doll, my plaything, and I was completely in control.

I started tapping, steadily, almost softly at first. A smooth double-time. But after a dozen or so beats I moved it up to a harder, more insistent tempo. Her breathing quickened, started to grow close, to almost, maybe, match my beats with the lacquered stick. I watched her stomach rise and fall, a background accompaniment, echo to her hisses and signs.

I moved, circled her breast and nipple with my stick, painting her with the beats. *Tap, tap, tap, sigh, sigh, moan, sigh.* Then the other breast, but a little harder this time. She started to glow, shining with gentle sweat. I could smell her, a thick rutting musk. Now she really was wet.

Now only her nipples. Each impact steady, sure, quick, and hard. She started to unconsciously twist her body, a little this way, then the opposite, to get away from the beats. For a moment, I thought about stopping. Make her stand up, make her get dressed, kick her out for such a show of life and independence, but that would mean I'd have to stop using this lovely new toy. The stick as well as SLUTSLAVE.

Then I did stop. Time for the next movement. She lifted her head, looking long at me, breathing heavy and hard. Her eyes flicked with a bit of fear but more than anything, a kind of plea: *More.*

Back into the bag. Simple. When you have control, you don't

need gadgets, gizmos, fine leathers. Fifty dollars in the right hands, with the right toy, and you have all you need. I came up with a pair matching the first clip. Her eyes grew even wider, her breathing deeper and quicker. She knew what was coming next. I didn't have to say anything.

The right one first. I leaned down and held it there, open, threatening around her so-hard nipple. She looked at it, then looked at me. Again, fear, but more than anything a desire for me to let go.

So I did. Her guttural bellow peaked threateningly toward a scream but didn't as she swallowed and swallowed, hissed and hissed it back down into herself. I was impressed.

I kept the clip on. It was wonderful to watch it bob up and down with her steady, deep breaths. I could have watched it all day, thinking: *This is mine. This is mine. This is mine.* I could have, but I had another tit to play with.

Somewhere during all this, my cock had been confined, trapped in my pants. Turning to the other tit, I felt how very, very hard I'd gotten. But that would wait. I was in control here. Not my dick.

The other one. Again, I held it there, looming over a tight little point of nipple. Again, I let go.

This time a short, quick, honest scream blew past her lips. Sound was a concern, but frankly, I didn't care. This was good—damned good. She was a good toy, a good plaything. She was mine to do with as I wanted.

I watched her, making sure the pain of the clips wasn't too much for her. She whistled her breaths, in and out, belly rising and falling as she tried to accept, flow with, use, and enjoy what was happening to her nipples, breasts, and body. I liked to watch her, knowing that I was the cause of all this. Yes, my cock was hard—steel, stone, rigid—in my pants, but this was almost better. The bliss painting her body in shimmering sweat, making her pant and moan, making her clit twitch, wasn't something of mine that could ever go soft, ever come too quick. I could make her come and come and come again and never take off my pants.

Time for the next step. Both pins were in place, both nodded, dipped, and rose from their grips on her nipples as she squirmed against the pain. I picked up the chopstick again. "See this?" I said. She pulled herself up from her blurry rapture. Her eyes took a long time to focus. She looked, she nodded.

I tapped one clothespin, hard, sending serious shocks down through it into her already aching nipple. She squealed in shock, in endorphin delight. I did the same to the other, then back again. Back and forth. She was a wonderful plaything, a fun little toy. I enjoyed playing with her very much. Oh, the things we could do.

I glanced up at the clock. A qualifier of our time together rang in my mind. Just a few hours, she had said, to start. Time had flown.

"Listen to me," I said. Her vision was almost lost against the waves of sensation, but she managed to finally see me. "We're almost finished—for tonight, that is. But before we do, I'm going to fuck you."

She frowned past what was happening to her nipples, her tits, her body, her cunt. My words reached through it all and created a worry.

Not good to have my plaything in such a state. Time to demonstrate that I am in control, that for her, I'm the boss, I'm the Master—and she is merely a toy, and toys have nothing, not even a worry.

I reached into my bag at my feet, pulled it out, tossed it at her feet. "I said, I'm going to fuck you. My dick—right there in front of you—is going in your cunt. Do you have a problem with that?"

She didn't. The smell of her, the grin that flashed on her gleaming face, told me that. Her legs were already gently parted, the kind of reckless, unselfconscious display that only a plaything in the middle of a high-flying pleasure/pain/endorphin rush could have. She may have had a worry, but she was more a hungry cunt. A wet and ready cunt. A wet and very ready cunt with a rubber dick on the floor in front of her.

"Pick it up," I said, though I didn't have to, not really, "and fuck yourself with it."

She bent forward, picked it up. Parting her thighs a bit more, she showed me her pink wetness. The bare thatch of hair that descended from her mons was matted and gleaming with juice. Her lips were already gently apart, swollen and ready for my store-bought dick.

I knew I could probably have fucked her with my own cock, or simply unzipped my fly and stuck myself into her hot, wet mouth. But that would mean I was flesh and blood, a man, and not the Master I really was. A Master is cold, a Master knows what to do with a plaything, a toy, a doll. I knew what to do. That's what I lived for: that dominance, that authority, that control.

She slipped the dildo into herself, just an inch to start. Then out, then in deeper, with a slow twist. She bit her lip in concentration, she closed her eyes in bliss—lost to the pain in her tits, the cock in her cunt.

Kneeling on my rug, legs very wide, she fucked herself. The gentle part ended quickly. She was now really, strongly fucking herself. A soft foam rimmed her cunt where the plastic slicked in and out. Some of her pubic hairs streaked along the length on the outstroke, curled in on the return. The hiss that had been only from the clips on her nipples was joined by the deeper sounds of a rolling, approaching come.

I didn't know her that well, but a good Master knows the sounds, no matter the toy, and I could tell that she could see it coming, could smell, taste it coming. Her breathing broke, became shorter, panting. *Now, right now,* I thought as I bent forward and put thumbs and fingers on the pins. I pulled.

Her eyes snapped open, fear lighting her irises. This time she didn't say, without words, *more,* but rather *Oh my God.*

I pulled. Not hard, just enough to drag her orgasm out, draw it farther out. Her fucking had slowed, eased, but she was too far along to stop. She couldn't if she wanted to.

I didn't want her to. So she didn't. I didn't need to say it, she understood it: the language of Master to SLUTSLAVE. Her fucking increased, pushing herself back up to the precipice. It didn't take long for her to be looking down the fast slope to her come. This time she said, without words, *now.*

Yes, SLUTSLAVE: *Now.* The pins came off. Screw noise concerns. Her scream came from her nipples, her tits, but also from her spasming, quivering, quaking cunt. Her come rattled her, making her body shake and her head bob back and forth. Her legs, already tensed from holding her forward, collapsed, spilling her backward on my old scratchy rug.

I watched her. Her breathing, after a long while, eased to a regular, resting rhythm. Then I went to my bathroom, got a big fluffy towel, and draped it over her. She didn't say anything, not even thanks.

I got her a glass of water from my kitchen, even put a little slice of lemon in it. She took it with gently quivering fingers. Drank all of it, handed it back. Then she said, "Thanks," but for the glass or the evening I didn't know.

Slowly, she got up, started hunting for her panties. I helped her, handing them over to her. She seemed to be happy.

Finally, she was dressed, though she looked funny with her hair messed. "Are you okay to go home?" I asked her, my hand on her arm. "Should I call you a cab?"

"I'm—whooo," she breathed, laughing for a second with a shivering after-feeling. "I'm okay. Really. Thank you," she finally said. "That was a blast."

"I'm glad. I'd love to do it again some time—soon."

"So would I. Really." Her hand was on the doorknob.

"Write me," I said, holding it open for her. "Send me a message and we'll pick a date."

"That'd be fun. Sure." She walked down the hall. When she got to the end she turned, waved to me. I waved back.

I checked my messages an hour or so later. Nothing. I watched some television, something I barely remember. Cops, I think. Or doctors. Something like that. Before I went to bed, I checked again. Nothing. I sent her a message: "Hope you had a good time. Write when you get a chance."

In the morning, nothing. I browsed some of the chatrooms, even though I'd never known her to be there that early. Nothing, of course.

When I got home from work I checked again. Spam. A few messages from some friends. Nothing. She's just busy. Things happen, I told myself, not believing my own thoughts.

Before I went to bed I wrote another message. But I didn't send it. Maybe in a few days, I thought.

I checked again the instant I walked in after work. Nothing. Nothing at all. I wrote her, against my better judgment. Simple, direct: "Concerned about how you're feeling. Please write."

That will do it, I thought. That'll reach her. Was it too much to ask? I thought she had fun. I thought she did.

But when I went to bed there was nothing but more spam, a few other messages. Nothing from her.

Around midnight, late for me, I went to bed. Nothing at all. I tried to masturbate but it didn't work out.

Eventually I fell asleep.

In the morning I checked again, first thing. Nothing. Nothing at all.

I never used the handle MASTER017 again.

WILD CHILD

Matt Conklin

Sex on planes is stupid. These people think they're so cool for joining the "Mile High Club." They probably think that sneaking a joint makes them oh so rebellious too. Whatever. Fucking on airplanes is overrated. They're just dumb conformists who want to do it because they read about it in a magazine. I just want to get to L.A. already. This whole thing is stupid....

I couldn't help looking over her shoulder. She was sitting right next to me, after all, and I've never been one not to notice a woman, even if she is fifteen years my junior. But even if I weren't the type to try to see what my seatmate was reading or check her out, the furious way this girl was scribbling in her notebook, a loud, angry kind of scrawl, was the equivalent of pounding a piano keyboard, hard, and it was difficult to ignore.

Her entire aura was angry, and she was dressed in typical

post-teen fashion—black tank top over jeans, with a black hoodie, plenty of black eyeliner, an eyebrow ring, and a scowl. Oh, and dark green Converse sneakers. As I took in her words, I knew immediately that she was all but a virgin. She was too fired up, too cocky to have ever fully surrendered to a boy—or a girl. She had all the charm of a young woman whose sensuality is hidden not so deeply beneath the surface, but who just hasn't figured it out yet.

She made me want to smack some sense into her, or fuck her. I could've told her to grow up, but what would be the point? So she could become jaded, I mean, "mature," like me? No, I figured I could have some fun with her, though, and maybe let Miss Attitude know that there's more than one way to get screwed on an airplane.

Her eyes, once you got past the shaggy bangs and overdone makeup, were almost sexy. And yes, I was now officially a dirty old man, likely twice her age or damn close, for even considering what she had going on under that hoodie. But she started it, and I felt like it was in both our best interests to pursue it.

"You're wrong, you know," I said in as snotty a voice as I could muster. Like meets like and all that. "It's not just about yuppies sneaking off for a quickie and calling it the best sex of the year. There are all kinds of ways to fuck on a plane. You're just too young to know about them."

She glared up at me, and let me tell you, it was the sexiest glare I'd ever seen, the kind of sneer that says "Leave me alone" and "I want to suck your cock" at the very same time, the kind of stare that made my dick even harder. "Like you'd know," she muttered, then cut me with her eyes before turning to face the window, deliberately closing her journal and curling up into a ball as best she could within the confines of the seat. Normally, I don't care what my neighbors are reading or eating or doing on a plane; I'm intent on getting where I'm going as quickly as possible. I've had my share of fun on planes, but for the most part I think they're utilitarian vehicles, the fastest way to get from point *A* to point *B,* nothing to get too excited about.

But I was excited about this girl, because she was definitely a girl, not a woman—not even close. I'd been spending my time with women who'd been around the block, who knew exactly how to give a blow job designed to make me melt, who approached sex like a sport they'd already won several medals in. Maybe that's not totally fair, but I was bored. I was on the plane because I wanted to shake things up, not necessarily with a wild fling, but with something different. I'd been certain a quick trip to Miami would snap me out of my rut. I'd fantasized about somewhere more exotic, but time was even tighter than money and I just wanted to be in the sun, soak up a few rays, ogle some chicks in bikinis and flirt and drink and not think about my latest breakup or my job performance. Things were salvageable at work, but I wasn't exactly going to be made employee of the year. I'd been drinking too much and had taken some of my frustration out on Heather, who'd finally had enough. But looking at this girl full of smoldering sex appeal buried beneath layers of goth indifference, I wondered if maybe I didn't even need to get to the land of beaches, sunshine, and Cuban flair for that to happen. This wild child seemed tailor-made for that, and looked like she could use someone to talk some sense into her before she became jaded like all the others.

Just then the stewardess came by and asked about drinks. My companion surprised me by ordering a club soda. I opted for water—with extra ice, and a whiskey. I smiled politely even as my mind formed deviant plans. My seatmate continued to pretend to ignore me, but I sensed her eyes peering at me over her shoulder. I pulled out a book, some thick thriller on the bestseller list I'd grabbed off the shelves. I used to have a stack of books just waiting to be read, and would sometimes rush home to them like they were old friends, but lately all I'd been reading were labels on jars and captions on my TV screen.

I tried to act like I was immersed in the book, playing hard to get, if you will, but when the stewardess returned with my requested cup of ice, I was grateful for the chance to pull out my tray, and grinned up at her. I think she thought I was flirting with her, from the way she leaned down, thrusting her tits in my face. That brief nearness made my seatmate a little jealous, apparently, because she scowled at the woman and demanded both a Coke and a tomato juice. "You better not spill on me," I said to her like she was eight.

"Why don't you just mind your own business?" she snapped back.

"Are you sure that's really what you want...Donna?" I asked, having copped a glance at the copy of *Bust* with its address label still attached she'd been rifling through.

"You're damn nosy, you know that?"

"You were the one writing about something that I happen to have a vested interest in."

"I was writing in my *journal,* you idiot."

"Fine. Stay young and uninformed, I don't care," I said, sipping the whisky I'd so wisely had the busty stewardess bring me. I reached for my book again and tried to imagine I was in first class. But my cock was insistent that I not let this one get away.

I ignored her for as long as I could stand it before turning toward her. She now had her headphones on full blast, her hoodie hiked up around her ears, and her body turned all the way away from me, her petite build allowing her to sit with her legs tucked against her as she faced the window, staring into the darkening sky.

"The ice is melting. Such a shame," I said quietly.

"Why?" She wasn't exactly gracious, but I was pretty sure I had piqued her interest.

"I don't know. Some people, you know, those stuffy, uptight dickwads you think so highly of, might be interested in playing with ice, like a sex toy. I'm sure that would be way beneath you, so there's no point in even going on about it."

There was silence for a few minutes as I sipped my drink and actually let myself get sucked into the mystery novel, the first clues making my brain spin with possibilities. Just when I thought I had a lead on who the killer might be, she spoke again. "Not that I actually care or anything, but what exactly would you do with the ice? And how do you do it without getting caught?"

I turned to look at her and her eyes seemed wider, the make-up seeming to fade as she stared up at me. "Well, the only real way to tell you is to show you. Otherwise it'll just sound boring. Do you think you're up for it? I'm not so sure a delicate flower like you could stand it. It's really more for the...masochistic sort of girl." Of course I already knew that she was as submissive as they come. It's the bratty ones who always need a good spanking, and the sniveling, simpering ones who are actually the biggest bitches once you scratch that outer layer. Time and time again, my theory has been proven right, as ballsy babes who've busted my nuts at work or among friends have begged to have their hair pulled, to choke on my cock, to be degraded in ways even I hadn't thought of.

Donna looked up at me and nodded. "I can take it." She said it like I was about to take her before a firing squad, rather than make her more aware of her nipples than she'd ever been.

"Try not to sound too enthusiastic," I said right into her ear. She shivered, and I made my lips brush against her lobe. "Cold?"

"No, I'm fine," she said.

"Good, because you're about to get a lot colder." And with a practiced move, I took one of the pieces of ice in my hand, put my arm around her, and quickly worked it below her T-shirt and into her bra. I made sure it was secure there, as I felt it start to melt just a little. I allowed my fingers only a brief meeting with her already-hardening flesh before removing my hand and patting her on the shoulder.

She looked at me again, her mouth open, fishlike. "Don't say anything. It's better that way. Just take deep breaths and focus on the sensation. And get used to it because I'm about to add another one," I told her. Her face could not have looked more shocked. Having ice melting against your nipples is one of those things you can't really prepare for. Even if you think you know what you're getting into, the reality is more painful, chilling, and exciting than you could have expected.

"Yes, there's going to be another one...unless you can tell me you hate it. Can't stand it. Wish I hadn't done it." The more I talked, the faster the words bubbled out, the stiffer my cock got. I'd wanted to try to play it cool, but I was just as aroused as she was. Initiation should be its own fetish, its own niche in the world of sex. Watching a woman go from barely knowing where her clit was to realizing that her nipples were way more sensitive than she'd thought, and could take all sorts of torment, was as beautiful as watching the glorious sunset going on outside our window.

"No. I mean, I can't say that. I don't know...I wouldn't say I like it, but I'd be disappointed if you didn't do it again."

"How disappointed?" I asked, stroking her cheek with one rough thumb.

"Well...I'd think you were a big, mean bully," she said. Now she was just toying with me.

"But would that really be such a bad thing?" I asked her before reaching down to pinch her icy nipple. She let out a sigh, then a hiss, as I manipulated the ice through the fabric of her T-shirt and hoodie so it was more directly in contact with her nipple.

"Oh, Donna, this is only the beginning. Because in a little while, I'm going to hand you three pieces of ice and tell you to go to the bathroom and insert them inside your pussy. And yes, you're going to do it, then walk back here, sit down, and make a big puddle in your seat. It's going to look like you've peed your pants. You're going to almost wish you *had* peed your pants, that it had all been an accident, because even though the ice is cold, your pussy's going to be on fire." I let my words sink into her stubborn little brain.

"But what about you?" she asked, clearly stalling for time.

"What about me?" I asked back, even though one look down at my crotch revealed just how hard this discussion was making me.

"I mean, why do I have to be the one to suffer? Don't you get to be iced up too?"

"Oh, little girl…" I said, then reached between her legs so she could feel my heat and I could feel hers. "There's so much you still have to learn. That is, if I'm not boring you by being a, what was it…?" I paused and shifted my fingers. "Oh yeah, a 'dumb conformist,'" I said as I pressed my palm flush with her pussy.

"No, you're not. You're not, I promise. I didn't know," she said, then clutched my arm tightly.

"What didn't you know, Donna?" I asked calmly as I plucked another piece of ice out of the rapidly melting pile and put it in my mouth. I held it between my teeth and smiled at her, waiting for her answer.

"I didn't know it would feel this good, or that I'd get so

turned on. I've only been with one guy, Rich, my ex-boyfriend. He was always all about the in-and-out—he said anything fancier was dreamed up by people with nothing better to do, who were never going to change the world."

"Ah, my dear, that's where you're wrong. If anything's going to change the world, it's going to be sex." I pried her fingers off my arm. "I think you need some more ice cubes," I told her.

She didn't object, didn't shrink away or glare. She watched, her eyes glued to my hand, as I took another cube and quickly slipped my hand down her shirt and into her bra, dropping my little gift, then extricating myself. My wet fingers dripped onto her neck as I massaged it.

"Now you," I said. "Rub it directly against your nipple. Think about what I could do if I had you alone, your breasts hanging out of your bra, your nipples straining in the air." Silently, she held one hand over her breast, using her hoodie to massage it into her. "After that melts, it'll be time for you to go to the bathroom," I whispered. She didn't say a word, but her shudder said it all. If you're tuned in to body language, a careful movie-watcher, a reader of the book of humanity, you can tell a shudder of horror from one of pleasure. They are oceans apart, gestures similar only in name. This shudder said, "I never thought it could feel this good. I don't care that we're on a plane, who knows how many feet in the air, in public, strangers. I just want more." Watching Donna was a pleasure all its own, a visual feast as my words and fingers coordinated to untangle her, unwrap her, unleash her. I, too, was changing, from dirty old man to enraptured seducer, her pleasure humming through my body as if we were attached by a wire.

"I bet you're very wet right now. I bet you're not thinking about how fast this plane is flying so it can get you to Miami and away from me."

"No...I'm not." There was a pause, while I breathed against her neck, out, then in, inhaling her scent, musky and flowery at once. "I like this," she said quietly. It was a simple statement, and from someone else might've been a small admission. But from her, it was everything. I had her. I cupped her pussy once more through her jeans, grinding my palm against it. She sunk lower in her seat, pressing back against me.

I leaned over and pressed my forehead lightly against hers, kissed her cheek softly. Kissing on planes is highly underrated. My lips met the soft skin of her cheek and I was reminded of just how young she was, her skin perfectly smooth, so tender I could practically sink right inside it, full of promise. I was too old for her in real life, whatever that was, but here, on this plane, I didn't mind making her feel hot and cold and aroused and wanted for a little while. She turned toward me and our lips met tenderly, like two teenagers making out in a movie theater, even as the ice wet her shirt and her pussy begged for more.

Her tongue insisted on entering my mouth, though her movements were small and tentative at first. I let her explore me before grabbing her hair and shoving my tongue into her mouth, as quietly as I could, the invasion swift, decisive. I knew our fellow passengers had to notice something amiss. It's hard to ignore two people in the throes of passion; even if you think you're not listening or observing, those telltale shifts, those familiar sounds rise up into your consciousness. I reminded myself that for all these people knew, she was my wife—my very young trophy wife, with me cast as the dirty old perv.

I didn't mind though, and when we broke apart, panting, I held my hand to her lips. She kissed each finger in turn, then unbuckled her seat belt and slithered over me, making sure to pause when her legs were straddling mine, a look on her face that, for a moment, made me question whether she was, indeed, as innocent as I'd painted her in my mind. She reached into the cup of ice and grabbed a handful, then winced as the shock of its cold sting greeted her. Then, still poised above me, Donna took a piece of ice and traced it over my lips, making them tremble, then part. She pressed it against my tongue and it felt heavy, solid.

She didn't want to be in charge, I could tell, but she wanted to at least let me know she could be. Then she turned and walked toward the back of the plane.

I swallowed hard. When she'd been right in front of me, I could easily let myself forget our surroundings. With her gone, I tried my best to stare straight at my hand, examining imaginary hangnails, my cuticles, my skin, memorizing the hairs on my knuckles. I was embarrassed, a new emotion for me. I didn't ask myself whether it was wrong to corrupt her, whether I should have waited for some other clueless kid her age who'd maybe banged one chick to show her what she was missing.

I was too horny for that. Her virginal yet knowing body was already haunting me. It had been, what, five years—or maybe more—since I'd been with a girl who was truly innocent, almost ignorant, about sex. Showing her not only how to please me but especially, how to please herself, the uses for her cunt and her clit and her nipples and her mouth, even the simple act of stroking the back of her neck: that's what I wanted to do for Donna.

All of a sudden, I knew she was on her way back. I turned around and saw her practically limping. She had done it; she'd really done it. Until that moment, I hadn't been totally sure, hadn't trusted that she was a) curious enough to continue and b) able to get those cubes into her pussy. Cunts don't exactly welcome freezing cold objects, but hers had. She walked around me and sat down, a look of heaven and torture across her face.

"You're an asshole, you know," she said.

"Am I? Really?"

"I bet you're single. I bet all your girlfriends break up with you."

She was taunting me, teasing me, and despite knowing better, it worked. I reached between her legs, feeling the cubes threatening to pop out. She continued to try to badmouth me, but I knew she was just putting up a front. I knew from the way her hips lifted against my hand, the cold wetness alive against my fingers. I didn't even feel that sorry that I couldn't slide my way inside her just then. I could have, but I liked the tension between us, liked seeing her react, almost despite herself.

"I think it's time for a nap," I said, smiling at her wickedly as I took my wet fingers and brushed them against her cheek. My index finger roamed over her lips. She let me inside, only to bite me, and I gritted my teeth. There's nothing I love more than being bitten by a woman in the throes of ecstasy, when she hardly knows her own strength, and wouldn't care if she did. I could tell Donna was a biter. And a screamer. And a gusher. Don't ask me how; I just knew.

"Take it back," I said. "What you wrote before. Take it back and maybe I'll make you come." I could see *I don't need you to make me come,* flash across her mind, but she didn't say it.

"I guess you were right," she managed.

"You guess?" I asked, letting my hand rest against her neck, lightly, but with the promise of more.

"You were right, I see that now. This is exciting, it's not what I'd thought it would be."

"Neither are you, Donna," I said, and leaned down, pressing my lips against her forehead. Her skin was warm there, and I rested like that for a moment before telling her to reach down and fish out the cubes.

"What?"

"You heard me. I want them. I'm gonna eat them."

That seemed to be the most shocking thing I could've told her. I wanted to eat the melted ice cubes that were in her pussy. I would be tasting her by proxy, but she would have to touch herself to make it happen. "I'll guard you," I said, and shifted in such a way that she'd be hidden from full view. She didn't protest anymore, just reached down and shifted enough so that she could retrieve the cubes, which were about half the size they'd been earlier. Water streamed down her hand and onto both of us. "Put them in my mouth," I instructed her.

She did as commanded, our eyes meeting as her hand and the cubes entered my mouth. The truth was, I wanted to devour her: lick her all over, keep her naked in my apartment overnight, or, hell, for a week. But I let her fingers slip out, before taking them in my own and this time, settling a magazine across her lap and a blanket across mine, before delving into her panties with both our hands, mine atop hers. I steered her and guided her, letting her fingers show us both what felt good.

"I've never…"

"I know," I assured her. This was a hell of a place to start, and as fluffy white clouds raced by our window, I taught my own sexy wild child how to masturbate: how to make herself come, how to touch her pussy in a way that could transcend any number of bouts of bad sex or heartache. I stayed with her as she trembled, turning her face into my shoulder and leaning toward me.

She asked for my number, but I didn't give it to her. I didn't want to totally tame her wildness, and I figured this was like that "if you give a man a fish…" saying. I had taught her what her body was good for; now it was up to her to go out and use it. That's not to say it was easy to step off that plane and feel the culture shock of heading back to my real life, where wildness was certainly in abundance, but never paired with such innocence. I let her use my sweater to wrap around her waist, where a big puddle sill remained.

I hope Donna learned a good lesson that will make her a better lover, to herself and others, someday. I learned that you're never too old to learn new sex tricks, and that sometimes it's the least likely strangers, on a plane even, who can show you a new side of yourself.

BRIANNA'S FIRE

Amanda Earl

Noah lifted his baton slightly, and the guest solo violinist raised her bow. He tapped the baton once more, and she played the opening to *Adagio for Strings*. With a sweep of Noah's hand, the cellist and pianist joined in, soon to be followed by the rest of the orchestra.

This was what he loved about conducting: the perfection of having gifted musicians follow his directions, and turning their individual sounds into one glorious piece of music, seducing the audience with his firm control.

The violinist opened up on stage. She put her entire body—mind and spirit—into that performance. Observing her release to the audience and to him excited Noah. Her music was haunting and sublime.

During rehearsals that week things had been very tense between Noah and the violinist. He had given her instruction, and she had refused.

"Just listen to this piece, Brianna. You're playing it as it's written. Let me hear your own interpretation. I know you can give me more."

"Maestro, I have tried. I have practiced, but this is the best I can do."

The two of them spent hours together after rehearsal, trying to perfect her technique. He brought in other interpretations of the performance, but it seemed as if she wasn't listening. Her ears took it in, but her mind and spirit did not.

"Brianna," he said late one night after the frustration was growing, "let's get a coffee."

They talked that night, for the first time. She told him all about her life in London, the boyfriend she'd left behind.

"He was so weak, Noah. He never seemed to make decisions or take control."

"Is that what you want then, Brianna—a man to control you?" Noah's voice grew husky.

Brianna lowered her eyes and blushed. "Sometimes I think that is exactly what I'm looking for." She looked directly into Noah's eyes and a shiver passed between the two of them.

Noah's pulse quickened. This wonderful, sensual woman, so intelligent and feisty...he imagined her just for one moment in his arms, then on her knees at his feet. His cock stirred as he looked back at her.

The room was silent except for the beating of his heart. He took her hand in his and turned it over.

"You have beautiful hands, Brianna. That's surprising in a violinist."

"I want them to be soft, Noah, not calloused. I want to be able to give gentle touches."

The next rehearsal went better. It was as if the sharing of secrets had brought Brianna out of her shell. She was less timid. When Noah told her to try something, she did so.

At the party afterward, he'd removed his bow tie and tuxedo jacket, and was sampling his favorite champagne when Brianna approached him. During rehearsal, she had worn casual clothes. He had definitely found her attractive. How could he not? She was beautiful: long red hair, cobalt-blue eyes, and soft pink lips. Her dress now looked elegant, yet feminine: black as ebony, but camouflaging softness within.

"Noah, I just wanted to thank you for tonight. I don't think I've ever performed so well."

"You're welcome, Brianna. Those late nights really paid off, didn't they?"

"I'm so glad to have had this opportunity to play for the orchestra...to play for you." Brianna's eyes were as dark as the Irish Sea in a storm. Noah smiled and took her hand, holding it for just one second longer than was appropriate.

"I was impressed by the way you were able to let yourself go, Brianna. Not all performers can do that."

Her pupils darkened and grew as she breathed in quickly, which showed Noah that he had aroused her. Noah allowed his own breathing to quicken, to show her that he too found her attractive. He was a firm believer in communication without words.

"Yes, Noah, perhaps you do bring out the best in me," Brianna said quietly.

"Why don't we get you a drink?"

"Thank you, Noah. I would love..." she hesitated, "I would love a very dry martini."

Her voice was mellifluous. She could have been a singer. He kept his eyes fixed firmly on hers. He'd already noticed the curve of her firm breasts through her dress, the nipples visible through the thin fabric, a slender waist, and soft, glowing skin. He breathed in her mesmerizing scent of violets.

He focused on Brianna for the rest of the evening, ignoring fawning patrons and sycophantic orchestra staff. This woman was different, fascinating, funny. They developed a crackling dialogue of repartee, playfully arguing. When he advanced, she parried, often with a subtle flick of wit.

He had a knack for revealing a woman's secrets, getting her to confess all, but Brianna told him very little. He knew she was from Ireland, but had spent most of her life in England, training at the London Music School. She had just done a stint with the City of London Philharmonic, but changed the subject quickly when he asked why. Soon the evening had to come to an end, as they had an early rehearsal the next morning.

"Look, you can't say that Cirque du Soleil is just a mere circus act. It is so much more, Noah."

"Ah, Brianna, if I'd known it was so easy to entertain you, I'd have brought out my magic act."

"That sounds like a wonderful idea, Noah. I look forward to that, but in the meantime, admit that they are a very sensual troupe. Their performance is filled with beauty."

"Sorry, Brianna, I'm just not a circus fan. I'd rather go to a good opera than see a circus."

"Opera? The sound of a woman caterwauling in as many languages as can be squeezed into one piece of music? Oh please, Noah."

"Well, perhaps one day, you'll accompany me to *La Bohème*. You'll see sensuality and sadness beyond anything you've ever seen. I guarantee. If not, you can make me go with you to one of your circus freak shows."

"I'd like you to come with me to see Cirque du Soleil, Noah. I want to see the smile on your face when you realize I'm right."

"Let me escort you to your car," he said. "I think you and I would disagree on just about every subject." He walked her over to a dark green Citroën.

"It does seem that way, but I do enjoy debating with you," she said, and paused, as if she wanted to say more.

"And I, you. But wait until I've taken you to an opera—you'll be struck dumb by its beauty."

He knew at this point that, if he were inclined, he could have suggested he accompany her for a nightcap, which would ultimately lead to sex, but that wasn't his style. Brianna was more than just a casual romp, and anyway, one-night stands held little interest for him. He needed much more, and perhaps she was the one to provide it.

"Good night, Noah. I'll probably toss and turn, thinking of a reply to your last gambit."

"Have a good night, Brianna. I hope you sleep well. I'm looking forward to our continued debate."

Brianna smiled and got into her car. Noah walked away, the scent of violets lingering from their touch.

That night, Noah felt restless and impatient. He knew he had to calm himself. He decided to go to an old hangout, Cris et Chuchotements. It was a fetish club with regular BDSM nights. He no longer frequented these kinds of places. He was used to slaves who knew just what he needed, but with Brianna on his mind, he had to be very, very patient, and he needed release.

He walked through the golden door, greeting the doorman, who still remembered him as a regular visitor. Noah descended the red-lit staircase into the dungeon, his cock beginning to harden as he contemplated the night's surprises.

He walked into the salon.

"Noah, how wonderful!" said a woman in the back corner.

Noah greeted Magda, his first slave. She had long, golden hair. Her curvy, voluptuous body was wrapped tightly in a red corset and short skirt. He could see the curve of her divine ass. He remembered the red marks he used to leave there with his first whip.

"How can I help you, Noah?"

"I thought I'd sample the wares a bit. I need a distraction."

"Did you want one of the women for your use tonight, Noah?"

Noah looked at Magda, and thought about taking her again, but too much history had passed between them.

"Yes, Magda. And make her a tall redhead, would you?"

Magda left Noah to think about Brianna while he waited. Brianna had sought him out, and this always excited him. She didn't expect him to come running for her. He would never do that, but he was definitely interested in her. He thought about the ritual they were embarking on. It was more than a court-ship ritual. It was the dance of master and slave. He would not seduce her, she would come willingly, learn to understand and accept her own needs as a woman and a submissive.

Noah remembered the advice of his mentor, Lord Collum, who had an eye for detecting and drawing out submissiveness in a woman, and who taught Noah as much as he could during their training sessions.

"Noah, if you really pay attention to a woman, she will give you clues about herself, and her sexuality. Her own perfume of musk and spice indicates arousal."

"What about a submissive woman, Regent? How can I tell whether a woman will submit to me?"

"Noah, we've got a long way to go before you're ready for that. Lots of training, but here are a few indicators: Intelligence and honesty are certainly essential. She has to enjoy the roles and rituals that go along with putting her into sub space. And she has to communicate her feelings of discomfort and pain at all times. A submissive has to be a strong and self-confident woman."

"Isn't that a paradox?"

"Not at all. She has to be strong enough to be open, to push herself further. She has to be self-confident enough to know that yielding will not take away from her strength."

"But aren't I just commanding her, and she just obeying?"

"Well, yes and no. Once you have established trust, you can dominate her, but a submissive has to have good instincts. She has to learn whom to trust. Also, she must always make the decision to yield each time. You must never take her submission for granted."

Noah thought about Brianna, the way she'd responded to him. Being around a maestro exhilarated her, breathed life into her. A dominant could be the air to a submissive's fire. Noah already knew that he wanted to be the air to stoke her fire.

Magda brought in a very beautiful woman named Colleen. She had long, auburn hair, tied up in a bun with tendrils hanging down the back of her short, clingy black dress. She was a businesswoman who was paying dearly for the chance to be dominated for the night. He was happy to give her this fantasy. And she was just what he needed.

He took her down to the whipping post in the dungeon, and practiced his whipping skills on her. Did it turn him on to have a woman tied up and at his mercy, awaiting the strikes of his whip? Absolutely. But even though his cock was hard, this wasn't about sex. It was about control and limits. He had his own limits. He was careful with this woman, giving her what she wanted, and taking what he wanted in return. She had been quite the screamer when she came with the flogger handle inside her, her ass covered in red marks. He needed those marks on her ass. He needed her screams. He could have come inside her, but instead he let her show gratitude by taking him in her mouth and paying homage to his cock. It felt so good to have the redhead at his feet. He imagined Brianna there. He was going to find a way to put her there.

It was an exhausting yet exhilarating session, and all he wanted to do was get home to his bed afterward, despite Magda's attempts to persuade him to share a drink.

"Another time, Magda," he said, and left the club.

Finally he'd be able to sleep. As Noah got ready for bed, he imagined Brianna doing the same. He knew she'd be thinking about him as she disrobed. He'd planted the seed, but not too forcefully. He had not pressed to see her socially. It was up to her to come forward now.

Noah's dreams that night were full of the long, lithe Brianna. He heard her violin playing, the soundtrack of her release, in his dream. He placed a forest-green, crushed-leather collar around her tender neck. Her hair was braided with hemp rope. He had seated her in a chair, her nipples pointed forward. Noah affixed her ankles to the chair legs with the thin rope. She winced slightly as the cord bit into her soft flesh. This made her lean forward, and her breasts jut out even more. Noah caressed her arms before placing them behind her back and tying them together with softer flat rope.

A woman bound is one of the most sensuous things in the world. She is completely vulnerable. Noah took this vulnerability seriously. He would never violate the trust so freely offered by a submissive. Brianna's large eyes and parted mouth reflected her arousal.

He kept her mouth ungagged. As much as he enjoyed seeing a woman strain and moan against a gag, he wanted to hear that beautiful voice cry out when she came. He gently unrolled a purple silk scarf and tied it over Brianna's eyes, wrapping it loosely so that she remained unharmed. The idea was to heighten her sensations by restricting her vision.

Noah's cock hardened as he gazed down at Brianna's glistening and bound body, but he steadied himself to ensure that he maintained control. He counted his breathing to even it, causing his erection to calm down. He took a feather and teased it gently over Brianna's long neck, onto her collarbone. A frisson of goose bumps decorated her breasts, arms, and stomach. He allowed the feather to trace her nipples, which stiffened in response.

She was tied but still able to part her legs further. Noah noticed her open cunt glistening with the onset of her juices as she yielded to him like a slice of ripe melon. He slid the feather gently over her thighs, and then carefully pressed it against her clitoris, which tightened and swelled as the feather moved insistently against it. Brianna pushed her pelvis up and down in time to Noah's feather. He kept his rhythm on her clit, gently stimulating her, but not taking her over just yet.

"Open your legs, Brianna," Noah said.

He watched Brianna's legs part wider and wider, straining against the ropes. "Oh, God, Noah, I'm going to come."

"Wait, girl. Don't come yet," Noah said while continuing to gently tease her clit.

"Please," she begged.

Noah gently inserted his index finger into her open cunt. "Now move, Brianna. That's a good girl."

Noah watched as Brianna lifted her hips up and down and felt her suck his finger in deeper.

"Not so fast, girl."

Brianna slowed down. He inserted a second finger, and she moaned in frustration.

"Oh please, Noah," she cried out, and her teeth bit hard against her lip.

"Beg for me. Beg and I'll let you come, girl. Do it now."

"Please, Noah, I'll do anything you tell me. You can do anything you want to me, just please, oh please, sir, may I come?" Her words burst out in short, breathless sobs.

He knew exactly how far to push her. It excited him beyond belief to have this kind of power over a woman. It was time.

Noah whispered the words in Brianna's ear, "Yes, slave, that's right, you will do anything for me. And now you are going to come for me, Brianna, come for your master."

Noah watched as Brianna let go. Her body relaxed, but her cunt tightened up around his fingers. These were the words she'd needed. And he was the one to give them to her. He could provide this release for her. He was a strong wind, and she, the embers. Sparks and air mingled and culminated in flame. She came hard, her juices flowing over his hand.

He awoke from the dream completely aroused. In reality he knew that it would take much more than that to get Brianna to the stage where she would come on demand for him.

The phone beside his bed rang.

"Hello," he said, still out of breath from his dream.

"Noah," Brianna said, her voice clear and sexy first thing in the morning. "Would you like to have breakfast?"

Brianna had passed the first test.

FORCEFUL PERSONALITIES

Dominic Santi

From the moment I first saw Christa, I wanted her naked and kneeling at my feet.

Looking was easy. Getting her to submit took some serious negotiation. She was wearing a power suit and doing her level best to fleece my start-up company into providing a cut-rate contract for the corporation she represented. My cock twitched at the sight of her shoulder-length blonde hair brushing against hand-tailored silk that complemented the almost startling blue of her eyes. Her breasts were full, firm mounds. She had the most perfect ass I'd ever seen.

It wasn't long before the innuendo in our conversations showed we both knew we were discussing a private as well as a public deal. Sparks flew between us with every offer and counteroffer. Christa made it clear she was only interested in doing things my way if it got her what she wanted. And she was willing to play dirty. She had a habit of chewing her lower lip that kept me so hard I would have been embarrassed if I were the type to blush at an erection.

I wasn't. Apparently, neither was Christa. She couldn't keep her eyes off my crotch. Each time I caught her looking, she just closed her jacket over the aroused points of her nipples and sucked on that full, red, pouty lip. Then she smiled and went back to business.

Two days later, I was so horny I swung the negotiations to an agreement that gave her more than I'd planned, though it still turned a tidy profit for me. The initial gut punch of meeting her had progressed beyond a simple hunger. I wanted her willing, and I wanted her for good. The day we signed the contract, I ratcheted our private negotiations to the next step by convincing my new colleague to join me for a celebratory dinner.

Christa told me I didn't need to pick her up—or open doors or choose the restaurant where we were going. I told her I did, keeping my hand firmly on the small of her back as I guided her into Alberto's, where I'd requested a secluded, candlelit table in the back. She was dressed for sin in a short, backless, skintight black knit sheath that showed off the delectable curve of her ass. No obvious panty lines. No garter bulges where the seamed black silk stockings rose from her four-inch strappy heels and disappeared under a hem that was barely a hand span below her crotch. The dress was cut low enough in front to show the cleavage between firm, high breasts I had no doubt would fit perfectly in my hands. She wasn't wearing a bra. However, when I looked closely, and I did, blatantly, I saw the almost imperceptible line at her waist telling me she was wearing a very tiny thong.

"You're gorgeous," I said as the waiter showed us to our table. When I moved my hand against her back, her nipples hardened. My hand slid lower, rubbing the string of the thong. I was done with innuendo. "You're overdressed."

"Thank...I beg your pardon?" She turned so fast she tipped on her heels. I steadied her and pulled out her chair for her.

"You heard me."

The look on her face was priceless as she slid into the chair. Ignoring the waiter, I leaned forward and spoke softly in her ear. "The dress is perfect. Take off the panties."

I moved past her to take my seat and turned my attention to the waiter. Christa's eyes flashed as I told him to bring me the wine list and two glasses of ice water. As soon as the waiter was out of earshot, Christa tapped her fingernails on the tablecloth and gave me a look that had brought Fortune 500 CEOs to their knees.

"What makes you think I'm taking my clothes off for you?"

I wasn't going to be the one kneeling. I handed her a napkin. "I'm going to be your lover, eventually your husband. The sooner you're naked, the sooner I'll give you orgasms."

I didn't expect Christa to let that pass unanswered either. But from my position, I could see the waiter returning with the water pitcher. As she drew in her breath, the waiter reached her side and picked up her glass. She snapped her mouth closed, biting her lip and drumming her fingers on the table as he filled our glasses. I covered her hand with mine, stroking my middle finger in her palm while I rubbed my thumb over the back of her knuckles and ordered my favorite wine. Eventually, her hand relaxed and she smiled tightly.

"You have quite the little fantasy world going there." She pulled her hand back as the waiter again left us. "Do you suffer such delusions often?"

I caught her fingertips and lifted her hand to my lips. "I believe in making fantasies come true." I kissed her fingers. When she shivered, I sucked the tip of her index finger into my mouth. Her eyes softened as a beautiful blush crept up her cheeks. I bit lightly, then sucked again, smiling as she once more set her teeth to her beautiful, full lower lip.

"I'll stop anytime you want, anytime you ask me to. All you have to do is say 'no' or 'stop' or 'don't.' " I ran my teeth over the full pad of her finger. "Trust me, Christa. I'm going to make you beg me to take you, and I'm going to make you come so hard you scream."

"This is ridiculous," she muttered, blowing her bangs off her forehead. But she didn't move her finger from my lips. Each time my teeth touched her skin, she shivered.

"It's sexy." I kissed her fingertip and set her hand back on the table.

The dining room was filling, but the light was low and tables nearest us were still empty. I took an ice cube from my water, trailing it over the exposed upper curves of her breasts.

"What on earth?" She grabbed my fingers, her eyes flicking quickly around the room to see if anyone had seen us.

I shook my head. "We want each other, Christa. What others think doesn't signify."

For a moment, she chewed her lip. Then she smiled and dropped her hand back to the table. The melting ice was running down over her skin and between her breasts. Her nipples were pebbled like rocks, the wet fabric clinging like a second skin as she shivered again. When the ice was almost gone, I dropped it into her cleavage. This time, when she touched her tongue to her lip, she licked slowly and sensuously.

"I don't know why I'm letting you do this," she whispered as the waiter appeared again. I left my hand against her breast.

"You're letting me pleasure you because it feels good, and because I'm going to make you come like you never have before. Don't move." Although the waiter didn't bat an eye, Christa flushed and looked away. I ordered for both of us, looking only at her as I carefully eased the top of her dress lower. I tucked in the edges of the damp fabric until her nipples were barely covered. When the waiter left us again, I picked up another ice cube.

"Tell me you want me, Christa."

The waiter was seating another couple at the table in back of Christa. With my hand innocently against the edge of her dress, I slipped the ice inside, so it rested on the top of her nipple beneath the clinging fabric. Christa gasped. The man being seated turned toward us. I ignored him, keeping my eyes on her more wildly flushing face as the wet circle grew over her breast. When the man turned away again, I picked up another piece of ice. I held it in my hand over her other breast.

"I dislike waiting, Christa."

I wanted her so badly I would have waited forever, but I wasn't going to tell her that. Instead, I watched the pink tip of her tongue flick in and out as she worried her lip. My cock was so hard I had no doubt the front of my pants was as wet as the front of her dress. Her skin was warm beneath my motionless fingers. She shivered as the water from the melting ice dripped onto her. When the waiter walked past with the drinks for the other table, she took a deep breath and whispered, "I want you."

I slipped the rest of the ice cube onto her nipple. She shook as I smoothed the folded top of her dress back into place.

"The sooner you obey me, the sooner you'll receive your pleasure. Remember that."

Christa nodded as I stroked the back of my fingers down her cleavage where the water had run. Her skin was cool to my touch. I knew my hand felt warm.

"Go to the restroom. Take off your panties and throw them away. Keep the top of your dress just as I have it."

Christa hesitated only a moment. Then she nodded and got

carefully to her feet. She didn't bother looking at the rest of the room. The beautiful, strong-willed woman I wanted so badly I hurt just smiled, turned, and walked slowly and seductively toward the hall. With each step, her hips swayed with a practiced gait that let me know she had made her decision.

By the time she returned, the ice had melted, leaving her dress clinging to her pointed nipples. When she was seated, I rested my hand where her stocking met the bottom of her dress, and I rewarded her with a slow, wet kiss.

"I'm proud of you, Christa." The tablecloths at Alberto's were long enough to hide a multitude of sins. I slid my hand over the top of her stocking, then over the even silkier skin at the top of her thigh. Then higher.

"Was it difficult to obey me?"

The neatly-trimmed thatch was slick with her juices. She shuddered as my fingers slid into her slit. With a soft moan, she slid forward on the seat.

"It was harder than hell." Her eyes closed as she sucked her lip between her teeth. "It was worth it."

I laughed softly, my fingers pushing deep into her cunt as my thumb settled on the protruding nub of her clit. I rubbed in slow, firm circles. When she gasped, I curled my fingers toward her belly button and rocked my hand.

"Come for me." My voice was harsh, but I couldn't help it. I nearly came in my pants watching her.

Fortunately, the first quaking shudder was almost immediate. The other tables were filling, and the waiter was approaching with our food. Christa was still trembling when I pulled us both up. I smiled indulgently at her bemused look as the waiter served us and quickly left. Christa gasped as I once more quietly slipped ice cubes over her nipples. Then I picked up my wineglass and proposed a toast to all our forthcoming mergers. Christa clinked her glass to mine, and with her eyes still smoldering, dug into her dinner.

I was tempted to insist on having dessert, for the pure pleasure of watching her face as I licked chocolate mousse off her fingers. But now that Christa had decided what she wanted, the naked desire on her face had me so hard I could wait no longer to get her alone in the car.

The waiter was too well trained to comment when I asked for a cup of ice to go. I tipped him handsomely. Then I slid my arm around Christa's shoulders and guided her out through a room now full of people who were much too busy to notice the passing of any two individuals.

It took Christa a minute to finesse her heels and that short skirt back into my car, though she was much less concerned about letting me look up her skirt than she had been on the way to the restaurant. When we were finally in, I opened the small container of ice. I took out two pieces, wetting them briefly in my mouth. Christa gasped as I slipped them in the now familiar positions on her nipples. When I picked up a third cube, she raised an eyebrow at me. I grinned and closed my palm around it, until water dripped out the side of my hand.

"Slide down in the seat and spread your legs."

She hesitated for only the briefest second. There wasn't much room, but the sight of her hiked-up skirt and the tops of her stockings framing her naked, well-trimmed pussy, was something I would take to my grave.

"I can't believe I'm doing this!" Her laugh was shaky as she slid down against the butter-soft leather. "I love it. Ooh!" Her eyes closed as I slid the ice down and up her slit, then back to circle the hypersensitive nub.

I put her hand on the ice, then directed her fingers to continue stroking in the same, slow, lazy pattern. With my left hand, I started the car. The familiar high pitch vibrated through me. "Keep circling."

Aside from the impeccable food and superb staff, one of the pluses of Alberto's was that it was less than ten minutes from my home. I pulled the car into the driveway and pressed the button to close the security gate behind me. I parked under a secluded tree on the far end of the circle and cut the engine. My cock throbbed at the glimpses of Christa's pussy as she swung her legs out. I grabbed some condoms and lube from the glove compartment. Then I took her elbow and steered her to the gazebo at the side of the house. I dumped the packets on the bench and sat down hard beside them.

"Straddle me." I pulled Christa roughly over my legs and onto my lap. Balanced on her high, teetering heels, she was just the right height. I yanked the front of her dress open and sucked a cold, turgid nipple into my mouth. She muffled a scream in her hand.

"Don't." I pulled her hand from her face. "I want to hear you come." Then I turned my head and sucked in the other nipple. It wasn't long before her moans became sobs and her hands were fisted in my hair, holding my head to her as she ground her naked pussy against my pants.

When her groans were almost constant, I urged her up enough for me to open my fly, shove down my pants, and free my cock. I grabbed a condom and a couple of lube packets. Then I pulled up her dress and guided my cock to her pussy lips. Her cries were desperate as she gripped my shoulders.

I lifted my lips from her nipple long enough to growl, "Fuck me!"

She instantly obeyed, inching her feet forward for balance. I sucked her nipple back into my mouth. I kept sucking, alternating from one nipple to the other while I guided her hips with one hand and diddled her cool, slippery clit with the other. Orgasms rolled over her in waves as her cries grew louder and louder.

I wanted more. I wanted all of her. And I wanted her to crave it. As the next waves rolled through her, I kneaded her bottom, squeezing and caressing until she finally pushed back against my hands. Then, I slowly pulled her cheeks apart.

"Turn around. I'm going to fuck your ass."

For just a moment, Christa stilled. Then she took a deep, shaking breath and looked me right in the eye.

"I've only done that once before. It hurt."

I twitched my cock inside her. "Do you believe I'll hurt you?"

Again, the slightest hesitation. Then she shook her head. She rose up and carefully moved her legs over me until she was straddling me facing the other way. Bracing her hands on her knees, she slowly sat back, lowering herself until she was positioned over me. I emptied an entire packet of lube over my latex-covered cock. Christa jumped when I smeared the slippery gel over her anus. She jumped again, gasping, when I pressed one well-slicked finger inside, then another. She moaned in pleasure when I slowly moved them in and out.

"That feels good," she whispered, shivering as the fingers diddling her anus stretched her sphincter open. With my other hand, I held myself firmly against her.

"My cock will feel better."

She gasped as the slippery tip started in. I put both hands on her hips and eased her to me. "Slowly, Christa. Finger your clit. That's it. Keep your fingers moving, no matter what."

Her bottom was cool from the meltwater that had run down between her cheeks and she was relaxed from her climaxes. As her weight settled onto me, my cock head slid slowly through. She gasped so loudly it was almost a cry. For a second, her whole body trembled. Then she moaned, long and slowly, as I pulled her down and my cock slid in to the hilt.

"OOH!"

The hot, tight spasms milking my shaft were sending me over the edge. Her fingers moved frantically between her legs as I set my hands on her waist and slowly fucked her ass up and down over my cock. Christa's cries were desperate now, pleading with me to fuck her ass hard and fast, begging me to make her come. Her shudders were almost continuous as her quivering ass sucked the orgasm through my cock.

I thrust up hard, shouting her name. She screamed and ground against me, her pussy juice squirting as she teetered on her shoes and I spurted load after load of hot, creamy spunk up her quaking ass.

I fell back into the seat, holding her tightly. Christa collapsed against me, her head resting on my shoulder as she shook and panted. When her breathing finally turned to nervous giggles, I smiled.

"Holy fucking hell!" She laughed, snuggling back into my arms. She sighed as my softening cock slid slowly free. She glanced down at the dress bunched at her waist. "I can't believe I just did that—and I'm still wearing my damn dress!"

"You told me you weren't taking your clothes off for me," I said.

"That was silly of me," she laughed softly. "You have my permission to take my dress off me, anytime you want." She turned and kissed the side of my face. "Sir."

I grabbed the front of her dress and tore it from her in one sharp rip. Christa giggled and snuggled deeper.

I kissed her shoulder softly. "We'll keep a small dressing room with your clothes for work and outside social occasions. But otherwise, when you're home, you're going to be naked, submissive, and supremely well fucked."

Christa sighed, but she didn't move to get up. "I suppose this means your bossiness is here to stay?"

I laughed and swatted her bottom. "It always has been."

She put her teeth to her lower lip. The gears were wheeling again. "What about my heels and my stockings and my jewelry?"

My cock jumped. I bit the back of her neck. "You can keep those."

This time her chuckle was low and contented. "Deal." She picked up the remnants of her dress and walked naked toward the house, her hips swaying seductively in the moonlight. "It's good to be home."

All I could do was laugh. My Christa had definitely been worth the wait.

VERONICA'S BODY

Isabelle Gray

Veronica has a past. She refuses to talk about it. Veronica is married to Vince. Vince is a particular man. He likes what he likes, wants what he wants. When he's unhappy Veronica is unhappy. He doesn't ask about her past. She does whatever it takes to make him happy. It is a mutually beneficial arrangement.

At night, Veronica sleeps chained to the bed she shares with her husband. Her slender wrists are cuffed together and then locked to the canopy above with a long length of chain, the better for her to sleep. Just before midnight, Veronica washes her face, brushes her teeth, performs her other evening ablutions. She dabs a bit of perfume on the points of her collarbone. As she goes through her routine, her stomach flutters and a flush of heat starts crawling across her skin. When she's ready, she takes a deep breath, slips out of her silk robe and lies on the bed where Vince is waiting. He stretches himself along her body, covering her thighs with his, the hair on his legs tickling her. Slowly, he drags his fingers between her thighs, traces her pussy lips, presses his hand against her mound, then up her torso, flat and firm. As he lowers his lips to her breasts, she gasps, every time. He sinks his teeth into each nipple, rolls the soft flesh between hard enamel. He kisses the hollow at the base of her throat, the tip of her chin, her armpits. He licks lazy circles along the undersides of her arms. Finally, he places a moist kiss on each inner wrist before fastening the cuffs around them and chaining his wife to the bed. He tells her to sleep well. He turns off the light and settles in next to his wife, a possessive arm draped across her stomach. He falls asleep smiling.

It doesn't matter if she's tired or not. Come midnight, Veronica knows that her place is in bed, by her husband's side. When they travel, the cuffs come with them. On the nights she can't sleep, Veronica lies in the dark, staring at the ceiling or out at the night sky, enjoying the mild ache in her arms, eyes wide open. She has lived a lot of her life with her eyes wide open.

Sometimes, a few hours after she has fallen asleep, Veronica feels her husband climb atop her, his cock hard and insistently throbbing against her thighs. She knows what to do. She spreads her legs, wide. As Vince buries his cock inside his wife, stretching her open, she moans drowsily. She doesn't have to move or groan or call out his name. She only has to allow herself to be used. It turns her on that in the dark of their bedroom, their bodies heavy with sleep, she is just a tight warm space from which her husband will extract his satisfaction. She is always wet and ready for him. Vince fucks her hard at night, moaning with each thrust of his hips, squeezing his fingers roughly into her thighs, leaving coin-sized bruises for her to admire in the morning.

Veronica has a life of her own, a successful career. She works long hours, keeps her own money. But she is always available to her husband. When he comes to her workplace with that look in his eye, his chin set to the right, she knows to close her office door behind him. She knows to speak only when spoken to, to fall to her knees, cross her ankles, bow her head. She stares at the shine of his shoes, the fine cut of his slacks. She bows her head lower, until she is prostrate. She lovingly kisses each of his shoes. She stays like that until she hears the zipper of his slacks slowly being lowered. He wraps his fingers in her long red hair, curling them into a tight fist. He pulls her head up, drags his thumb across her lower lip, then slides his thumb into her mouth. She sucks on it, loudly, sloppily. He opens her mouth wider and says, "Take me," with an edge to his voice. She extends her tongue, leans forward slightly, inhales deeply as he fills her mouth with his cock. At first, he holds himself there in the silky warmth of her mouth, her jaw aching as it accommodates his girth. Then he grips her head with both hands and rocks his hips, slowly fucking her mouth the same way he fucks her cunt or her ass or her tits, as Veronica rakes her fingernails along the undersides of Vince's ass and down the backs of his thighs.

Veronica likes the reminder that the life of her own comes with strings attached. She gags around his cock at first, but then her throat muscles relax and she allows herself to surrender, to let herself be used. She curls her tongue along the underside of Vince's cock, enjoying the texture of him. After Vince comes, he casts his eyes downward. Veronica straddles his feet and lowers herself until her pussy grazes the leather of her husband's shoes. She wraps her arms around his legs, and sighs as Vince rests a gentle hand atop her head. She starts sliding back and forth, her pussy getting wetter, her clit slick and throbbing. The closer she gets to coming, the faster and harder she grinds. Her thigh muscles strain; they tremble. She is always sweaty, her clothes clinging to her body as an orgasm rolls through her, radiating out from her cunt to every end of her body. She kisses Vince's shoes once more. She smells herself on him. After he leaves her to the rest of her day, she gathers her composure and slips back into the life of her own.

Vince and Veronica met when he saw her as a patient in the emergency room. After setting the broken bone in her arm, he sat on the rolling stool next to the hospital bed where she rested and said, "I'd like to take you out sometime."

Veronica sat up and arched an eyebrow. "Isn't that against the rules?"

Vince smiled coldly. "I'd like to take you out sometime."

Veronica looked at her arm, freshly casted, and held it out. "Give me your number," she said.

Two weeks later, Vince took her to an Ethiopian restaurant. They ate *wat* with *injera* and drank wine. They talked about everything and nothing. Toward the end of the meal, without ceremony, Vince said, "I am a man with brutal appetites."

Veronica was quiet. She had known all kinds of men, many of them brutal. Vince was the first to acknowledge his desires so frankly. She eyed him carefully—his thick black hair, roughly chiseled features, cold blue eyes. She decided she could love this man who knew himself so well, stated what he wanted so shamelessly. She could give him exactly what he needed to satisfy his appetites. Veronica wrapped her fingers around the stem of her wineglass and raised it toward him. Vince nodded, and explained in explicit detail what he would take from her. As she listened, Veronica crossed her legs, squeezing her thighs together. An unfamiliar warmth raced across her cheeks and down her neck. Her chest tightened.

When he finished, Vince said, "I'm not looking for a maid. I'm not looking for a mother. I'm looking for a body. I also know how to appreciate that which I am allowed to take."

Veronica reached beneath the table for Vince's hand, pulled it between her thighs. As he slid two fingers inside her, she looked right into his eyes and said, "That's important."

On their wedding night, Vince told Veronica that he didn't believe in punishment. He believed in discipline. Then he taught her the difference. He had converted the spare bedroom of their home into a discipline chamber with a St. Andrew's cross, a leather-covered paddling bench, and a sling hanging in the far corner. The wooden floors gleamed and the room was well lit. On one wall, there was a wide range of toys, some of which Veronica recognized, and others with which she would soon become familiar. As Veronica slowly walked around the room, dragging her fingers along each piece of equipment, Vince said, "I'll never understand why so many people believe this sort of thing should be done in darkness."

Veronica nodded, then turned away from Vince, asking him to unzip her wedding dress. As she stepped out of the layers of silk and lace, she said, "I agree." Then she stood against the cross, lowering her head. Her entire body relaxed as Vince fastened leather cuffs around her wrists and ankles, kissing the backs of her thighs as he worked his way upward. For a long while, Vince stood behind his new wife, inhaling her scent, letting his hands memorize the contours of her body. He cupped a breast in each hand and squeezed roughly, watching her flesh splay between his fingers. After twisting her nipples until she winced, her body arching into the pain, he pinched her nipples between a pair of clamps, connected by a thin gold chain.

Veronica felt drowsy. Her head lolled to one side and she smiled. Vince stepped away, and she felt a rush of cold air in the separation between their bodies. She shivered. Vince smacked her ass, smiling as her skin rippled beneath his hand. A blush of red quickly appeared. He smacked Veronica's ass again, harder this time, his hand stinging as it rebounded. "Discipline," he said, "is a reminder." Veronica's entire body tensed. The room was silent save for the sound of Vince's shoes as he crossed the room and eyed his wall of toys, selecting a few. He set his implements on the floor next to Veronica's body and picked up a long stainless steel paddle, with three rows of holes. He dragged the paddle across her shoulders and Veronica shivered. Then he raised the paddle in the air and brought it down twice in rapid succession. A darker shade of red blushed across Veronica's ass. She flexed her feet. A bead of sweat trickled down her neck and along her spine.

Vince began to smack Veronica's ass with the paddle in a firm and steady rhythm. Veronica barely had time to breathe between each blow. She closed her eyes, forced herself to relax, to fall into the pain. The harder Vince paddled her ass, the freer she felt. Then he stopped and dropped the paddle to the ground. She gasped at the clatter it made. Vince picked up another toy. He perched his chin on her shoulder and said, "Close your eyes. Open your mouth." She obliged willingly and felt something wide and rubbery in her mouth. "Get it wet," Vince said. Veronica lathed the foreign object with her tongue until Vince was satisfied. Then he spread her asscheeks apart and slowly worked what she now realized was an anal plug into the tight fissure of her ass. She could feel her body resisting, but Vince's will was more resolute than that of her body. Her body stretched around the plug, and after a short while, the sharp throbbing dulled into a pleasant discomfort. She felt swollen, full.

Veronica felt her head being pulled back, the muscles of her neck stretched to their limit. Vince slid his other hand from between her breasts up her throat, and he squeezed as he pressed his lips against hers, shoving his tongue between her lips. They kissed almost violently and, overwhelmed by the very burn of her skin, Veronica moaned into Vince's mouth. She thought, *I would say* I do *all over again*. She opened her mouth wider, nipped Vince's lower lip between her teeth. He pulled away for a moment and said, "Yes. I like that. Don't ever back down from me." Veronica leaned in, wanting more of Vince's lips against hers. He tightened the grip of his fingers in her hair, holding her lips a breath away from his. He followed the sensuous arcs of each lip with the tip of his tongue. He whispered that she was his whore and she whispered back, "Yes. Yes I am." They kissed again, harder this time, so hard that they could feel the bone beneath the flesh of their lips. Vince flicked his tongue against hers a final time, then brought his lips to her shoulder, first licking the salt from her skin, then sinking his teeth into her body. Veronica hissed, again arching into the sharp pain.

Vince reached down for a new toy, draped it over her shoulder. Veronica moaned, louder this time, as she felt several long strands of leather draping down over her breasts. Vince kissed the small indentations left by his teeth and took a few steps back. With a flick of the wrist, he let the cat-o'-nine-tails dance across her back lightly, just enough to tease. Another flick of his wrist, and a second dance of the whip came, a slow one. Vince draped the whip over her shoulder again, this time pulling it toward him, letting the tails drag down Veronica's back. He pulled his arm back, and without warning, released a vicious blow. Her entire body strained upward. Veronica clenched and unclenched her fingers. Another blow landed. Then came a steady rain of leather against her skin, the expanse of her back turning pink, then red, then a darker shade of red.

Veronica felt each blow down through her bones. After what seemed like hours, a thin sheen of sweat covered her entire body. Vince could see the streaks of the whip's tails in the perspiration. He threw the whip against Veronica's body until he could raise his arm no more.

"Do you understand discipline?"

Veronica nodded limply. "Yes," she whispered hoarsely.

Vince dropped the whip, gently released his new wife from her bondage and carried her across the threshold of their bedroom. He laid her in the middle of their bed and knelt between her legs. As he removed the nipple clamps, setting them on the night table, she cried out and shuddered, the blood rushing back to the puckered, sensitive nubs.

Veronica looked up at Vince and saw unexpected kindness in his eyes. "Have I pleased you?" she asked.

Vince finished undressing, then crawled back into bed, lying on his side next to Veronica. He slid one hand down her flat stomach and between her thighs and started stroking Veronica's clit with his thumb as he slid two fingers inside her cunt where she was wet and waiting for him. He pressed her clit hard and Veronica raised her hips, wanting more. Tears welled in her eyes. "Have I pleased you?" she asked again, her voice stronger this time. Vince slid his wet fingers into his mouth and savored the taste of her. Then he covered her body with his, buried his cock deep in her cunt. Veronica spread her legs wide. She clenched around him and Vince took a deep breath, tried to control himself. Veronica's entire body expanded, opening to her husband in every way he needed. Her ass continued to throb and pucker around the plug. She felt consumed. She arched her back, pressing her breasts against Vince's chest, enjoying the firmness of his body against hers.

Vince clasped her throat again, squeezing harder this time. "Look at me," he said.

Veronica opened her eyes and held her husband's gaze. She met each thrust, urging him deeper. Beads of sweat from his face fell into her mouth and she swallowed, trying to memorize the taste of his body. As she crested a new wave of pleasure and her body began its familiar descent into bliss, she asked one final time, "Have I pleased you?"

Vince reared back, holding the tip of his cock at the sensitive, quivering inner lips of her cunt. He squeezed Veronica's throat harder, and she wrapped one hand around his wrist. Vince thrust forward. Veronica cried out again, feeling a blade of pleasure so deeply, she thought her body might split at the heart. Vince kissed her chin, then her lips. The kiss was so soft it sent a frisson of pleasure curling around her spine. He stared at her for a moment longer. Finally, he said, "Yes."

THE LONDON O

Justine Elyot

It had swiftly become a matter of pride to Lloyd that he should provide more, bigger, better orgasms than any of my previous lovers and, in the early days of our relationship, I confess that I might have played on this tiny insecurity.

"Orlando was so well named," I teased over moules marinières in some Café Rouge or another. "An O at either end." I ran the point of my tongue over the tender morsel in its creamy broth-filled shell. "He had the gift."

"Either end?" Lloyd's light tone did nothing to fool me. He knew a challenge when he heard one. "You mean he gave you an orgasm in your toes? And the top of your head?"

"The location isn't important," I grinned, swirling the lascivious mollusk around the insides of my mouth before swallowing.

"Au contraire, Miss Martin, the location is a critical factor. Don't you agree?"

Lloyd sipped sagely at his red wine, his eyes narrowed, keen to pursue the conversational line.

"Well, without wanting to get too graphic at the dinner table…"

"Oh, no, I'm not talking body geography. I know the map of Sophie well enough, and I don't care how well-thumbed it is. I know where to plant my flag when I want her earth to move. I'm talking about places."

"Places? Orgasmic places?"

"Yeah. Where's the strangest place you ever climaxed?"

"Oh…well. A swimming pool. An underground parking lot. A hotel balcony." I frowned in an effort of memory.

"Tame stuff. Vanilla in the extreme. I'm surprised at you."

"Lloyd! Where am I supposed to do it? Onstage?"

"That would add spice." His louche grin was as wide as a wolf's, and his knee nudged mine beneath the checkered cloth. "I'm sure you'd find an appreciative audience."

"So where's your most outrageous spot for hitting the spot, then? Since you see yourself as the voice of experience here."

"There was a croquet lawn. A rowing boat. An aircraft hangar. And that was all before I left college."

"So what is the point you are making? Were those orgasms better?"

"No, they weren't better," he conceded. "But they had a quality all of their own. Didn't you find that with your experiences outside the bedroom?"

"I suppose I did. Yes."

"But nobody has ever pursued that with you?"

"No. I must admit, my past lovers have mainly wanted privacy. Don't you?"

"There's a time and a place."

I snorted.

"That appears to be the *opposite* of what you're proposing. You seem to be saying that any time and any place are fine for sex."

"Not sex necessarily. Just having an orgasm. Coming. Oh, I love that. Coming. Such an innocent word; such a coy little euphemism."

"Okay, now I'm struggling."

"You will be. Finish that up. I'm getting the bill. I need to show you what I mean and in this case, I think actions will speak louder than words."

I mopped up the last of the delicious sauce with a hunk of baguette and pushed the plate aside.

"Just coming," I said.

Outside it had begun to rain; Lloyd grasped my hand and held on to me, weaving me through the shining streets, between phalanxes of umbrellas, down to Soho, where the pavement narrowed and we had to maintain strict single file until we reached the forlorn last bastion of that district's seedy past. On Brewer Street, the red and blue neon flickered from the doorways; the rain conferred a strange and poignant glamour to the scene. Lloyd and I were frequent visitors to this historic fleshpot; I'm sure some of the patrons of the row of sex boutiques must have wondered if we had furnished our entire flat from their stock. I used to order that kind of thing online, but Lloyd converted me to the "experience" and the "ambience" and, most importantly, the exquisite, needling shame of handing my purchases over the counter. I both hated and loved it, but now I had the taste for it.

Through a rainbow-colored door curtain we passed, its plastic strips sliding coldly across our wet faces, into a brightly lit outpost of Sodom and Gomorrah.

"Evenin'," we were greeted laconically by the vast biker who presided over this empire of extravagant sin. Lloyd tipped his head and the man returned to his *Standard* without further interrogation.

"What are we looking for?" I asked Lloyd in a whisper as he led me beyond the lurid DVD covers and gnarly latex phalluses, even past the spanking and bondage section where we had spent many happy browsing hours.

"Knickers," he murmured, heading through an archway to a small square room populated by headless mannequins in PVC basques. Then he looked at me with a salacious smirk. "Whore's drawers."

"What's underwear got to do with it?" I wondered, having well and truly lost the connection between al fresco climax and these scanty scraps of hideous nylon.

"Hmm," was the only reply I got, Lloyd being now completely absorbed in the racks and shelves of cheap tartwear.

"Crotchless?" I hazarded, fingering a plastic peephole bra and slit panty set.

"Quite the opposite. No, not that…where the hell are they? I *saw* them here, I'm sure I did…aha!"

He wheeled around in triumph, brandishing a clear plastic bag containing what looked like an ordinary pair of black lacy briefs. But that was not all it contained. A remote control unit sat alongside the garment…remote-controlled knickers? *Oh!*

"I think I've heard of these," I said guardedly, stretching out a hand for further inspection. He handed over the bag, confirming my suspicions. Attached to the gusset at strategic intervals were a clitoral stimulator and a vibrator. "Are you serious?"

"Are you scared?" he taunted, taking the bag back and rustling it in my face, making ghostly *woo woo* noises. "Attack of the knickers!"

"They're expensive," I noted.

"I think they'd be worth it," he said, his voice a broken croon. He had that glazed look in his eyes that he always gets when he's imagining devilish and deviant practices. "Oh, the fun I could have with you...in these."

"So that's what you mean when you talk about odd locations for orgasms. In theory, I could have one anywhere at all...if I was wearing these."

"Yes. Anywhere at all. If I pressed the button...oh, the power! It could go to my head."

"I think it's already gone to somewhere else," I remarked, glancing down at his bulging trouser crotch.

As ever, it was my task to hand the purchase over the counter while Lloyd did the credit card bit. As ever, I crimsoned, prayed that no comment would be passed, no eye contact made. Eye contact, of a knowing kind, *was* made, but the comment was reserved for Lloyd.

"No returns, I'm afraid," he said. "Same as with all the other vibes. I'm sure you'll be satisfied with it though."

I was staring stonily at some massage oils, refusing to look up at their no doubt expansive grins and winks.

"Have you road tested one yourself?" Lloyd asked. *Oh, come on, let's go.*

"Yeah. I'd recommend it. Very quiet, no annoying buzzing. So you can wear them...anywhere."

"Thanks. I'll bear that in mind."

The shopkeeper was right. The vibrator unit was indeed almost inaudible, as I discovered on the tube journey home, having been persuaded to change my knickers in a pavement toilet cubicle before descending the escalator. Riding smoothly down on the moving staircase, past drinkers and diners and late-working office types, I was highly conscious of the difference. The fabric was snug and tight, so that the vibrator attachment was firmly lodged inside and the cold rippled latex of the clitoral stimulator nudged and rubbed exactly as advertised.

"How does it feel?" whispered Lloyd, standing beside me,

one hand placed possessively on my bum, rubbing my skirt as if this would wear through and reveal the answer.

"Very, very rude," I replied. "Wicked and indecent. I really hope I don't have some kind of accident on the way home. I do not want to end up in Casualty wearing these."

"Does it fill you? Are you wet? Does it rub against your clit?"

"Yes to all three. Shut up, for god's sake!"

"Oh, no, I want you to know you're wearing it; I don't want you to be able to forget. And I want you to know that I know. God, this is turning me on. I hope there aren't any delays on the Northern Line tonight."

We stepped off the escalator and I made a concerted effort to try and walk normally, notwithstanding the exquisite pressure on my clit and the large fake cock wedged in my pussy.

"It's giving you a sensational wiggle," said Lloyd admiringly, falling behind me to survey my swaying backside. "It looks so *obvious* that your pussy is stuffed. But I suppose I know it is, which makes a difference. Maybe nobody else would guess."

I was convinced that everybody knew it as we headed on to the platform. Every passerby, from the teenage youths clicking teeth and sucking back high-energy sodas to the elderly, suited man reading his *Telegraph*, was perfectly cognizant of the fact that I was wearing vibrating knickers, the crotch soaked, my pussy wrapped around a plastic cock, because I was a dirty slut who loves to come and can't get enough orgasms.

Lloyd kept putting his hand into his jacket pocket, teasing me with the fear that he might be about to activate the vibrator, causing me to clamp my thighs together and clench my pelvic-floor muscles. By the time the train came roaring through the tunnel, though, he had still not pressed the magic button.

The train was about three-quarters full, and we could not

find a seat together, so I sat in the center of one row while he took a place by the door, at the end of the opposite bank. Sitting like that, with a highly-perfumed lady on one side and a gay punk on the other, I was suddenly sure that people might be able to see up my skirt somehow, even though it was knee length and didn't even give away the fact that I was wearing stockings ordinarily. I decided to cross my legs, but this pushed the nubbed rubber even farther into my swimming clit and made my pussy feel even fuller, an inescapable sensation. I squirmed against the seat cushion, unsure whether to uncross my legs again, and Lloyd chose that moment to flip my switch.

I had to swallow a cry as the invasive presence in my pussy began to rev up, a slow shudder at first, speeding to an almost unbearable throb. It felt so painfully wanton that I knew my climax would not be put off for long. I sat back, stretching my spine, trying my very hardest not to pant or moan. My pussy lips twitched and my nipples were hard and sore, pushing against the lace of my bra until some of the pattern must have transferred to them. Lloyd's sly, delighted smile accentuated the hot rush of sensation; he had had to put a copy of the *Evening Standard* over his crotch to hide the excitement of it all. My nether regions seemed to be flexing and rippling beyond any vestige of muscular control; the vibrator whizzed up to maximum speed, my clit was swollen and struggling to barge past the little rubber stimulators, my cheeks were hotter than fire and I was fidgeting so much that my neighbors forewent the customary Tube etiquette of complete-oblivion-to-all and began looking sideways at me. And then I came, pressing my hands down into my lap, trying to breathe through the intense flood of liquid sweetness, shuffling my bottom against the cushion and biting down on my lip.

And we were still only at Goodge Street. It had taken less

than five minutes to make me come in public on the dusty up-
holstery of Transport for London.

The gay punk and the perfumed lady moved to the left and
right respectively, making no secret of their desire to distance
themselves. I couldn't blame them. I was sure the heavy odor of
my arousal and satisfaction must have been hanging in the air,
breaking the barrier of the woman's civet-drenched fragrance
and the gay punk's patchouli. I spent the rest of the journey
looking daggers at Lloyd, or as many daggers as I could muster
in the face of the great awe and wonder his sheer perversion
engendered in my spirit.

By the time we arrived at Highgate, it was clear that we
would never make the journey from the station to our flat
without Lloyd's cock punching a hole through his trousers. We
ran with our respective hindrances of an erection and a pair
of vibrating knickers as quickly as we could up the path and
into the wooded area that stood so conveniently at the side of
the Archway Road where the underground came overground.
Lloyd shoved me unceremoniously against the bark of a tree, my
breasts pushing against the rough wood, and hitched my skirt
to the waist, pulling down the back of the knickers to expose
my bottom to the fresh night air. Yards away from us, rail passengers mooched up and down the pathway, and the late night
traffic rumbled and lumbered. The nearby street provided just
enough low yellow light to give us a few visual clues as to how
to go about our swift and urgent coupling. Lloyd did not quite
pull the panties down, leaving the vibrator where it lay.

"I want your arse," he muttered, priming it with a thumb
that he had bathed in the juices of my overworked clit. "You can
keep that thing on. I'm going to switch it on now." Once more,
to my consternated delight, the stiff obstruction in my pussy began to buzz and throb, though the clit stimulator was only half

in place now, giving way to the more pressing issue of Lloyd's easy access. Once I was relaxed enough to take two of Lloyd's fingers in my tiny, tight hole, he decided he could hold back no longer, unzipping hurriedly and pushing his damp cockhead between my spread cheeks.

The vibe swelled and filled me as he eased the bulbous tip through my rear pucker. We moaned in concert; I from delirious fullness, he from long-anticipated relief. The farther in he slid, the wider and fatter and more apt to split I felt inside, until I had no sensation anywhere other than that seat of basest needs. I was a pussy and arsehole, full and well used, as I should be.

"Look at you," grunted Lloyd, once he was fully sheathed, his balls gently dangling against my lower cheeks. "Getting your arse fucked against a tree, with a full pussy. I bet Orlando never did that for you."

"N-no," I admitted, though my voice came out as a trickle of a quiver. "Oh. No."

"So who's the orgasm-meister now, eh?" He began to pull his shaft back, slowly, switching every nerve ending to its brightest setting on the way. "Who makes you come the hardest?"

"You do," I assured him, pushing my bum back, inviting him back in with all the urgency I could muster.

He was halfway along now, and I could not bear it if he pulled all the way out. I tried to clamp my muscles down on him, but it was difficult, and it stung.

"Who has the hottest, kinkiest plans for you, Sophie? Who knows exactly what kind of a dirty, nasty girl you are?"

"Oh, you, oh, you." He slammed back in and I hissed blissfully.

"Yes, me. Nobody else. Not fucking *Orlando*. Me. I'm the man for you."

He began to thrust hard, forcing my pelvis into the desiccated bark, the tip of his cock nudging against the rounded end of the vibrator with each uncompromising plunge into my rudest depths. I imagined the two cocks, real and simulated, joining together and making one long, pitiless invader, keeping that back-and-forth rhythm going from pussy to arsehole and back, forever and without end. The tree trunks here were narrow enough to wrap my arms around, and I clung on for dear life, hanging there while Lloyd gripped my hips and dug deeper and harder than I had thought possible. I knew I would be sore along there for a day or so, but I knew also that each shift and squirm in my office chair would make me smile and glow with the memory. The combination of the vibrator and the cock sent me into a roaring chaos of orgasm that I nevertheless had to keep quiet about, just as on the tube, for fear of disturbing the public. Lloyd froze behind me, then sent a long, sibilant hiss out through the trees before soaking my arse with his plentiful seed, sending jet after jet up, one after the other.

"God, you could have been made for me," he panted, his head on my shoulder for an exhausted moment, before straightening up and making himself decent once again. I could not quite make myself decent, still in the vibe knickers, which were becoming itchy and too wet to wear without an obvious slicking sound when I walked, not to mention a large stain spreading across my backside and sticking the material to my skin, but I somehow made it back to our flat, feeling that every passerby knew my secret and was giving Lloyd a knowing wink behind my back.

Still, we thought the new addition to our toy box a very valuable one, and the vibrating panties have had innumerable outings since their memorable debut. I wore them in the British Museum, on the London Eye, at the cinema in Leicester Square and picnicking in Hyde Park. They were always just the thing to brighten up a dull day, and we came very close to fulfilling Lloyd's ambition of making me come, hard and long, in every tourist attraction in the City. Most unforgettably, I began to sweat and puff in the middle of Buckingham Palace and had to sit on a velvet chair pulled out for me by one of the security guards.

"She's having one of her turns," said Lloyd laconically, winking at the man, before taking me out and having me down on the Victoria Embankment.

So when it comes down to the question of who provides more, bigger, better orgasms, Lloyd is the hands-down winner. He is also the hands-free winner. I really don't think Orlando will ever be able to catch up now.

PINK CHEEKS

Fiona Locke

Ever been spanked?"

Charles's question catches me totally off guard. "What?"

"You heard me, Emma. Have you ever been spanked?"

I've been so focused on my computer screen it takes several seconds for me to register what he's asking. "What, you mean as a kid?"

My coworker grins slyly at me. "Well, that too," he drawls, waiting for me to catch on. His bright blue eyes sparkle with mischief, making me blush. "No, later. When you grew up. The adult kind."

The truth is that I haven't, though I've always secretly wanted to be. But there's no way I'm telling *him* that.

I don't believe it. He's trying to make me confess to having kinky fantasies, but I'm not going to admit it until *he* does. Besides, it's too much fun playing dumb. "What are you talking about? Only kids get smacked."

Charles laughs. "Silly girl. I'm talking about the sexy kind.

The *erotic* kind. You've got to know what I mean."

Jolted, I peer over the top of our cubicle for a quick glance around the office. "Will you keep your voice down?" I plead, my ears burning.

He rolls his chair closer to me, and I tilt my computer screen away from him. He lowers his voice to a conspiratorial whisper. "Erotic spanking," he repeats. "That's what I'm talking about. With a lover."

I stare at him blankly for a moment, then feign illumination. "Ohh," I say. "I get it! You mean..." I shake my head and look away, laughing. A lover, indeed. Everyone knows the roses I got on my birthday last month came from the receptionist.

But he won't let go of his line of questioning. "That's right," he says, his eyes invading me with their frankness. "So you haven't done it, but have you ever *thought* about it?"

This is too much. I'm going to die of embarrassment if he keeps this up. "Have *you*?" I retort.

Now he glances at his computer, and I suddenly wonder what he's working on. Is he even working at all? Or just surfing dirty websites? I lean back in my chair and crane my neck around to see, but he quickly turns the screen away.

"Uh-huh," I say triumphantly. "Just as I thought. You know they keep a record of every website we visit, don't you?"

Charles dismisses my warning with a wave of his hand, but I happen to know for a fact that one of the guys in Human Resources was sacked last year for exactly that. He'd been downloading split-crotch shots from some busty bimbo site, saving them to his hard drive here at work so his wife wouldn't find them. I can't imagine Charles looking at anything that unimaginative, but still...

My words have had an effect, though, and he appears to be closing down whatever page he was on. He glances over at me with a cryptic smile. "Doesn't hurt to be cautious," he says.

I turn back to my own screen and furtively finish reading the story he had interrupted. One of the author's best, a little tale about a Victorian gentleman and his naughty maid. Squirming, I type a quick, appreciative response and then shut down the newsgroup. Websites aren't safe, but I can download the newsgroup posts with my email. They don't read our private correspondence.

I sense Charles watching me out of the corner of his eye. His interrogation has got my dirty mind working overtime, and I can almost imagine I'm broadcasting my thoughts to him. Can he smell my arousal?

Shifting in my seat, I force myself to get back to work.

"You still here, then?"

I glance up at the voice. Grant, always the last one to leave, is putting on his coat. Charles is still at work beside me in the cubicle. I must have lost track of the time.

"Afraid so," I sigh. "Got to finish this report."

Charles waits a beat before nodding. "Yeah. Me, too."

"Well, I'm calling it a day," Grant says. "One of you will have to lock up." He hands the keys to Charles, even though I'm closer.

Charles bids him a pleasant evening and an odd look passes between the men as Charles pockets the keys. I listen to the sound of Grant's footsteps moving down the corridor and out the front door.

Now my coworker turns to me, the cryptic smile on his face. "We're alone," he states. An insinuation. A threat. A promise.

"So we are," I say, forcing a cool smile of my own. "Well, back to work."

"Oh, no." He rises slowly from his chair and comes to me, reaching across me for my mouse.

"What are you—?"

Before I can protest, he's navigated his way to a master directory revealing the source and destination of posts from a newsgroup with a very conspicuous name. I gasp.

"My, my," he says. "What a naughty girl."

I blush furiously and look away. This is surreal. It's like a story straight from the newsgroup. There's no doubt in my mind what's coming next. And there's no question that I'll submit.

Charles takes me by the hand, and I go meekly where I am led. I don't lift my head until we reach the break room, which smells of tepid brown water and stale pastries. He guides me directly to the single wooden straight-backed chair in the room. The very same chair I've talked about with my imaginary friends on the newsgroup. It's the one I always use, squirming on the hard seat as I fantasize about the pain of a spanking. At last the penny drops.

"*Victorian Schoolmaster,*" I say in an awed whisper.

Charles gives me the evil grin he signs all his posts with. It's far more effective in person. "*Pink Cheeks,*" he replies.

I giggle, hearing my moniker aloud for the first time.

"This is no laughing matter, young lady," he says sternly.

My reply is automatic. "No, sir." It's how I've addressed him in writing numerous times. But actually saying it to him...I'm trembling with fear, anticipation, ecstasy, and a thousand other things there are no emoticons to express.

"You know what you need."

I'm not sure if it's a question or a statement, but I know how I'm meant to respond in any case. "Yes, sir," I whisper.

"Good girl."

A palpable silence follows. Enough time for all to become clear. "Victorian Schoolmaster" began posting to the group a few weeks after I did. So he must have known all along. That was months ago. I quiver at the thought. How many hundreds of posts have I made in that time? How many fantasies have I described in explicit detail? Worst of all—how many of his stories have I gushed over, declaring them my favorite masturbation aids?

I look up to see Charles peering intently at me, reading my thoughts.

"Oh, yes, my dear," he says with deep satisfaction. "I know all about your kinky little mind. I know all your hot buttons and trigger words. And I intend to make full use of that knowledge." He pauses before adding, "You've earned yourself a sound spanking, young lady, and you're about to learn what a well-smacked bottom feels like. You naughty, naughty little girl."

The words nail me one by one. He's a fantasy come to life before my eyes. I'd even been tempted to write about him on the newsgroup—a fantasy about my handsome coworker with the vivid blue eyes—but something held me back. Now I'm immensely relieved about that.

With slow deliberation he indicates the chair and I chew my lip. I know what he wants and I know better than to pretend I don't. Obediently, I place the chair in the center of the room and return to stand in front of Charles, my head down.

"Now then, little miss," he says, eyeing me sternly, just like the Victorian schoolmaster he plays so well online. "I think you know what comes next."

I do. As if in a dream, he seats himself in the austere chair, his trousers taut over firm muscular thighs. I stare at his lap, dizzy.

I sink into position and place my clammy hands on the floor. I never thought I'd be seeing the ugly yellow lino this close.

Charles's hand rests on my bottom and I am still, as though frozen by a spell. He pats me gently over my tailored skirt and then slowly begins to raise it. I lift my hips to help him tug it up over my rear.

"Naughty little girls," Charles says, "who read naughty little stories deserve to have their naughty little bottoms smacked."

I shudder at the words, blood rushing loudly in my ears as my heart hammers in my chest.

He caresses my bottom and I writhe over his knees, imagining his approval as he sees the panties I've described on the newsgroup. The ones that make me feel like a schoolgirl again. Without a word, he slips his fingers into the waistband of my white cotton knickers, pulling them down to expose me. I flush with embarrassment, my face burning.

Now his palm rests on my bare skin. The stifling room drops twenty degrees as the erotic dread consumes me. Helpless, I shiver and lie trembling across his thighs. For a moment—just a moment—I want to leap up and run. Call it off, scurry away, and hide forever. But I know I won't. I *can't*.

"Discipline, Emma," my stern schoolmaster says, "is something you clearly need. And I intend to teach you a firm lesson. You've had this punishment coming for a long time."

"Yes, sir," I moan. It's all I'm capable of saying.

Then I feel his palm lift from me. I hold my breath. The hand seems to hang suspended in the air forever before coming down to meet my skin with a loud smack. Startled by the reality of the situation more than by the pain, I yelp. Another smack, another yelp. Another and another and another. I'm feverish with embarrassment and desire as he spanks me briskly, thoroughly, not neglecting a single inch of vulnerable flesh.

"Blatant disregard of the rules," he chides. "And what has it earned you, young lady? A good sound spanking." A particularly hard volley of smacks punctuates these words and I cry out even louder.

When he finally stops, I moan softly, writhing over his lap. *Don't stop,* I try to tell him with my body. But he does. The warm glow in my backside is comforting. It matches the one on my face. He urges me up and I struggle gracelessly to my feet, unable to look at him.

"I'm not finished with you, my girl," Charles says. He waits for me to look up at him before adding, "Your hairbrush. Go and collect it."

I blush even more fiercely, now truly mortified. Of course. He knows all about that, too. The antique ebony one I found on eBay and described to the group in loving detail. I carry it in my bag and every time I brush my hair with it, I imagine a no-nonsense authority figure using it on my backside.

My hands are shaky and sweaty as I hurry to obey, fumbling the hairbrush out of my handbag and nearly dropping it as I present it to him.

Charles smacks it against his hand, making me wince. "Back over my knees," he orders.

My legs have forsaken me. I collapse into position.

He lays the cool wood against my burning flesh, and I utter a little mouselike squeak. He smoothes it over every inch of reddened skin, making me squirm even more. I close my eyes and brace myself. I've never even had the courage to spank myself with it; I have no idea how it will feel.

Charles taps it against my bottom. "Prepare yourself, young lady. This will teach you a lesson you'll never forget."

The first stroke connects and I arch wildly on his lap, crying out at the pain. He doesn't give me time to recover before delivering the next one, and the next.

I'm astonished at the pain. I never imagined it would hurt this much. I'd read and written about countless hairbrush spankings, but never truly understood the sensation. It's terrible and

wonderful at once, especially when I'm at the mercy of a skilled
and uncompromising disciplinarian.

I breathe into each stroke, hissing through my teeth, yelping
as the wood strikes my tender flesh. When I struggle, he holds
me firmly in place. I'm helpless. Delirious. Flying.

After a dozen strokes, he finally stops. I lie gasping and panting over his lap. I see him set my hairbrush down on the table in
front of me, and I melt with relief.

"Have you learned the value of discipline?" he asks.

"Yes, sir," I whimper.

"Good girl." He trails his fingertips over my punished bottom. Then he squeezes my burning cheeks, making me squeal.

He gives a soft laugh. Then he helps me up again. And sits
there, silent. Waiting.

I can't play dumb and wouldn't dare try. He knows me inside out. He knows every single element in my fantasy life, and
he relishes exploiting them. "Thank you for punishing me, sir,"
I say.

Charles smiles and rises to gather me in his arms, stroking
me like a cherished pet. His hands stray to my tender bottom
and he squeezes, making me yip.

"Pink Cheeks," he says fondly. "I think you'll be staying behind tomorrow night as well. And the night after that."

I bury my face in his chest, tingling all over with sensations
I don't quite know how to process yet. My first spanking. I can
hardly wait to write about it. I know my favorite imaginary
friend will respond.

HOW BAD DO YOU WANT IT?

Gwen Masters

I sat in the middle of the rumpled bed. The sounds of silence were all around me—the ticking of the clock, the call of a distant bird, the lack of footsteps in the hallway. Wayne had ordered me to stay naked, said he would be right back, and left me there. That was an hour ago.

My bare breasts felt heavy in my hands. The red marks on them were beginning to fade. Wayne had used the new whip, the one that bit like fire. I had closed my eyes and counted the strokes out loud, waiting for the moment when he would decide I had had enough. My wedding ring was cool against my over-heated skin.

Wayne liked suspense. He loved to hold the whip above my skin, moving it just enough to stir up the tiniest breeze, then bringing it down when I least expected it. He loved to lull me into a feeling of security, then test me by pushing the bound-aries. No one would know what I enjoyed just from looking at me. None of my friends knew the way things were. Only I understood that when I disappeared behind closed doors, being submissive wasn't just a desire, it was a need—it was what kept me ready to face the world.

Tired of waiting for him, I lay down and closed my eyes. I dozed on the bed until I awoke to the familiar crunch of tires on the gravel driveway.

Wayne whistled his way into the bedroom. He smiled when he saw I was still naked, just as he had left me. He sat on the bed behind me and snuggled close, pulling me back against his broad chest.

"I went to Blake's house," he said as he kissed my ear.

"How is Blake?" I asked.

Wayne's hand slid down my belly, seeking the place between my legs. I opened my thighs for him. When he spoke, his voice was sensuous and filled with promise.

"Blake is looking forward to seeing you, baby."

I sat very still. The tone of my husband's voice said all I needed to know, but it took a moment for it to sink in. Wayne said nothing else, just rested his lips lightly on my shoulder, waiting for the thoughts to form in my head. He knew I wouldn't say no—if Wayne wanted me to do something, I would do it. It was my pleasure to please him. We had never talked about having another man in bed with us, but Wayne wasn't one to let me know all that was on his mind, either. He liked surprises just as much as he liked suspense.

"I know you like him," Wayne said softly. "I've seen the way you look at him."

"That doesn't mean..."

"I've never questioned your faithfulness."

The silence fell between us. The ticking of the clock was very loud. Wayne simply sat and listened to it while he let me sort through my thoughts. There was an impossible jumble of them.

"Can I ask a question?" I said.

"Go ahead."

"Why?"

Wayne seemed prepared for any question I might ask, save that one. It took him aback.

"Why?" he repeated.

"Yes. Why?"

Wayne contemplated that while his hands slid up and down my arms.

"You know it doesn't make me happy when you question me."

"Yes," I said.

Wayne kissed my shoulder. "I could say it's about pleasing me. I could say it's about pushing you further than you've been before. I could say it's a test of your trust."

I nodded, waiting.

"It is all those things. But it's also a treat for you. Blake is your type, isn't he?"

The scarlet blush rose from my chest to my face, lighting me up with heat.

"You've never said it. But I've seen the way you get turned on when you read about a woman with more than one guy. I know how you get when I use more than one toy on you."

As he ran his hands up and down my arms, I realized Wayne knew me much better than I knew myself. Had the way I looked at Blake really been that obvious?

"You've never been into threesomes," I pointed out, shifting the attention from my actions to his. Wayne said nothing, and by doing so he acknowledged that he wouldn't let the conversation waver from the point. He kissed my shoulder one more time before he stood up from the bed. From the look in his eyes, I knew the discussion was over.

He left the room and when he returned, Blake was with him.

Wayne looked pointedly at the quilt I had pulled up over my body. Understanding what he wanted, I let it fall to the bed. My nipples immediately hardened.

Blake took a deep breath as he looked at me. I studiously met his eyes, unwilling to look lower, though every part of me wanted to see just how excited he really was. Out of the corner of my eye, I saw the slow grin on Wayne's face. He settled against the dresser and watched as Blake and I faced each other over the ten feet that separated us.

"You're beautiful," Blake finally said, and the blush that heated my face seemed to go all through my body and settle between my thighs.

My hand trembled when I reached out toward Blake. He stepped forward to take it. I looked back at Wayne, and he slowly nodded his head. In his eyes was an expression I couldn't even begin to read.

I pulled Blake onto the bed with me.

It was the strangest feeling, to have an unfamiliar man's body in bed with me. Blake was taller than Wayne. Where Wayne was stocky and muscular, Blake was leaner. Where Wayne had straight, short hair, Blake had curls that wrapped around my fingers as I pulled him down to kiss me.

Blake whispered something against my lips. It sounded like "Are you sure?" I kissed him deeply enough to leave no doubt that I was sure. It wasn't just about pleasing Wayne, though that was part of it—I wanted to please Blake, too.

Wayne abruptly pushed away from the dresser and came to the bed. He stood beside it and looked down at me. I met his eyes while Blake kissed a trail down my throat. Wayne didn't say a word. When Blake's tongue found my nipple, I let out a moan. Only then did Wayne blink and tear his gaze away from my face.

Then Blake was sliding his hand between my legs, and suddenly Wayne was the last thing on my mind. I arched up to him and silently begged for more.

"Tell me what you like," Blake said. I did better than that—I showed him. When I put my hand over his and taught him how to make me weak with pleasure, Blake paid attention. Soon he was doing it all himself, rising above me on the bed, looking down at my body as I lost myself in what he was doing. He kept it up, moving his hand in a steady, deep rhythm. The familiar tightening felt almost foreign this time, and I suddenly realized it was because a different man was doing the things that drove me wild.

I was staring at my husband when Blake made me come.

"Good girl," Wayne whispered.

Blake's cock was hard against my thigh. I reached for the buttons of his shirt. Together we pulled it off. When I unbuttoned his jeans, I was very aware of Wayne watching. I pushed the jeans down. The boxers underneath them hid nothing at all. Blake groaned from deep in his throat when I circled my hand around his dick and slowly stroked him.

"You're so damn good at this," Blake murmured into my ear.

When he started to move away, I followed him. On my knees, I opened my mouth and licked the head of his cock. Blake shuddered and ran his fingers through my hair. I looked up at him while I took him into my mouth, one slow inch after another.

Wayne's hand on my hip was like a jolt of electricity, making me jump with the surprise of it. He ran his fingertips lightly over my skin. His other hand slid up to my neck. He took my hair in his hand and moved it away, so he could see what I was doing to Blake.

"Do a good job, baby," he encouraged, and I sucked Blake deeper into my mouth.

Wayne's hand rose from my hip and came down, lightly slapping my ass. He did it a second time, then a third, until he had built up a rhythm. Each time his hand came down on my ass, I sucked Blake into my mouth. Between the spanks, I pulled back until he was almost free of my lips. When Wayne sped up, so did I.

"Fuck—fuck, I'm going to come," Blake warned.

Blake thrust into my mouth. I slid my hands up his hips and held him closer, encouraging him to go deeper. His legs trembled. His breathing became ragged. He said my name and then there was nothing but a long, tortured moan as he started to come.

The first shot of come had such force behind it, I almost gagged. Wayne ran his hands into my hair and held me steady. I couldn't back away—I had to take whatever Blake gave me. I sucked hard, swallowed again, and caressed his cock with my tongue until he pulled back with a satisfied sigh.

Wayne suddenly let me go. I fell sideways onto the bed and looked back at him. He was watching me with the tiniest smile on his face. He opened the nightstand drawer and pulled out the paddle.

"Get him hard," Wayne ordered. "Then ride his dick."

I stared at the paddle, then looked back up at Wayne. His face was calm and quiet, but his eyes gave him away—they were burning with desire.

I turned to Blake. He let out a pleased sigh as I began to suck on him again, stroking him to life with my tongue. It didn't take long before he was standing up straight, his erection proud and thick. He went willingly onto his back, and I climbed over him.

Blake tangled his hands in my hair as I kissed his throat. I worked my way over his chest, kissing him everywhere, teasing him down below by rubbing my pussy just over his cock but not letting him inside me. I kept it up until Blake's body was trembling with tension. Only then did I sit back on his cock, sliding him into me with one long, delicious thrust.

Just as I took him all the way in, the paddle came down across my ass. It was a hard, stinging spank. I gasped at the sudden pain of it.

"Fuck him," Wayne said. "Fuck another man while your husband punishes you for it."

Blake pulled me down for a kiss. All the while I was moving up and down on him. Each time I slid all the way down, Wayne spanked me with the paddle.

"Do you want to make him come?" Wayne asked. Blake was sucking on my nipples while I rode his cock. Wayne was spanking me with the paddle every time I came down.

"Yes," I said.

"Do you want him to come inside you?"

"Yes."

"How much are you willing to pay for it?"

I looked over at Wayne. My motion stopped. Blake looked up to see what had caused the sudden shift, and I heard his quiet gasp.

Wayne was holding a leather whip.

He lashed it against his palm. The red mark rose immediately, blossoming on his skin like a flower of pain. Blake's cock twitched inside me, harder than ever.

"Fuck him," Wayne said. "Make it worth every last stripe of this whip on your ass."

I looked back at Blake. His eyes were wide. He reached up to touch my face, brushed the hair back away from my forehead, and softly kissed my mouth. He took my hands in his, holding them tight, holding me steady.

"Fuck me," he whispered against my lips.

I rose up on his dick. Then I slid down, taking him all the way, focusing on the way he stretched me with every stroke. The whip whistled through the air and cracked against my skin, making me cry out. It stung like a line of fire poured across my ass. The second strike whistled down and this time I buried my face in Blake's shoulder. His hands tightened on mine, holding me down for the punishment I was earning with every thrust.

I rode Blake hard. I put all the force I had into the thrusts. Our hips slammed together. I fucked him hard enough to hurt, even while the whip came down again and again across my ass and my thighs. I was giving Blake pleasure, but taking equal pain for doing so. The combination was heady, the most twisted mind fuck Wayne had ever come up with.

Abruptly, Wayne stopped. Before I could turn to look at him, he grabbed my hair in his hand and yanked my head back. "Make him come," he ordered. "Make him come in my wife's cunt."

Blake didn't need much encouragement. He was right on the edge. When I sat straight up and took him as deep as he could go, he cried out with the pleasure of it. Wet heat flooded me as he arched up, pushing his body hard against mine, letting go into me.

When I caught my breath, Wayne was standing beside the bed, waiting. His clothes were gone. He was breathing hard. Blake slid out of me and I moved to face Wayne, silently asking what he wanted.

"Let me see what he did to you," Wayne said. "Lie down. Show me."

I lay down on the bed and spread my legs. Wayne groaned as he looked between them. Then he was on the bed, coming up between my thighs and driving home with one smooth thrust. His

fingers found my nipples and he pinched down hard. Blake sat
on the edge of the bed, watching with rapt attention as Wayne's
cock slid in and out of the same cunt he had just fucked.

"You're going to take my come too, aren't you?"

Wayne squeezed down harder on my nipples. The pain roared
through me, bringing tears to my eyes. That was what it took
to send Wayne over that final edge. He yelled out with pleasure
as he emptied himself into me. When he pulled out, wetness
trickled down my thighs. The sensation was delightful enough
to make up for the burning pain of my ass. Wayne sat on the bed
and looked at me until my breathing calmed.

"You didn't come." I shook my head. "That's all right. Blake
will make you come again. Won't you, Blake?"

Both men looked at each other. It was a question, but the
tone of it was more like a demand. I immediately recognized
the situation for what it was—if Blake was going to be a play-
mate for his wife, Wayne wanted to make sure he still had the
upper hand.

Blake picked up the whip. He touched the tip of it as he
looked it over. Then he slid it gently against my thigh, drawing
a shiver. He gave me a wicked smile.

"Absolutely," he answered.

STRIPPED

Clancy Nacht

'm naked and it's cold in the room. Very cold. It feels like a meat locker and for all I know, that's what it is. Hemp rope prickles my arms and I can feel it there, solid, holding me snug.

It's not just some cheap kidnapping, nothing so tacky as just being restrained. I am bound, bound head to toe by an expert, and I have been suspended from the floor.

I was not allowed to watch any of it. The first thing that he did when I answered the door to my apartment was to hold up a satin sash. It waved gently to tease my nose, and I giggled out of nervousness. I didn't know what this could mean.

John was always so mysterious, and I suppose I'd built a silly fantasy around him: who he was, what he'd be like. I read too many true crime novels, always projecting the worst that could happen to me. Still, with this gorgeous tall man, his pale skin and blue eyes, I can't help but be intrigued.

As soon as I stepped over the threshold and locked the door, he swept the sash over my eyes, leaving me blind but for the bright lights past the courtyard of my apartment complex. They were all so sleazy, those neon lights advertising strippers. It was just the sort of neighborhood that a true crime might happen in. That's why I'd moved there.

I've never had a death wish per se, but there is a certain thrill to taking really huge risks with your life. Even though I'd dated John and spoken with him, he'd never given away much about himself, seeming to prefer a long, slow courtship. I admit that I was frustrated. I'd slide my fingers between my lips, rubbing the middle one over my clit, imagining what his hands would feel like on me there. His hands were always so soft, but so cold.

One particularly adventurous night, I snuck out to the refrigerator to take an ice cube back to bed. The cold felt shocking on my cunt. I'd opened my lips up so that I could run the dripping cube between them, toyed with the hole. I'd never thought of doing it before, not before John and his long dark hair and cold hands. It tingled, cooled, brought sensations to the surface on such a fragile, hot part of my body that I almost couldn't stand it. Though I'd thought it might make my cunt go numb, it had the exact opposite effect. It made my whole body tingle, prickling with gooseflesh and sweat until I released it into myself, letting it slide slowly over the opening before finally pushing it inside of me.

It wasn't much, just a cube. It had melted down, but even the fact that it was inside of me was exciting. I supplemented my adventure with a mini–rocket vibrator. Running it over my clit again and again, I squeezed my thighs tightly, moving that sliver of ice cube inside of me, feeling it touching, feeling the cold liquid as it melted inside of me. It was amazing, thrilling, like I was being lifted off of the bed, moving to another plane of pleasure that rocked through my body, leaving me gasping. My cold fingers were on my breasts, pinching my nipples, and all I could think about was John.

John here in front of me, out in the courtyard of my apartment complex. I could hear the car horns in the street not far away. I expected him to lead me to his car, somewhere, anywhere, but he just stood there before me. I adjusted the strap on my halter dress, fidgeting with it nervously. I could feel his gaze. It made me feel small, like a child. I wanted to please him, but I didn't know how, didn't know what he wanted of me.

I turned my ankle in, balancing on a stiletto heel, feeling strangely bashful.

"I do not like that dress." John's voice seemed to carry in the whispers of the humid Houston air.

I reached for the blindfold, starting to turn. "I'll change."

"No." He was behind me, breathing heavily, arms around me as he started to unbutton my halter dress. It was yellow and flowing, girlish, maybe too girlish. I worried that he thought I was too immature to date. I hadn't known where we were going, and Houston is warm almost year round. Still, I cursed myself for such a silly choice right up until I felt his warm hands cupping me under the smocking of my dress.

The night was warm; his hands were cold. They were always so cold. But his breath in my ear was hot, and I could feel the heat of his erection behind me, pressing against my simple cotton dress. "Finish it," he whispered.

For a moment, I was at a loss as to what he wanted of me. He placed my hands on the buttons starting at the waist and I froze. "But we're outside."

"I want to see you now. I want to see you naked outside. I want to take in your beauty. I promise, we will not stay here long."

His words were persuasive, as were his hands. They'd slid down the front of my dress and under my cotton panties. They were so wet already, and I couldn't help being embarrassed. "You feel ready."

I blushed and turned my head, but as I couldn't see anything, I had nowhere to direct my blush. I merely whimpered and hoped I wasn't degrading myself by twisting around so that he would touch more than my trimmed pubis. His fingers brushed gently over my light down, and one finger slipped between the folds and out again. He brought that hand up and I could hear him sucking his finger. I was so aroused, I was shaking.

"If you want more of that," he whispered, "then take off your clothes."

It didn't take long to comply; I wasn't wearing much. The dress fell off my shoulders once his hands were out of it and I wriggled my wet panties down past my hips, where gravity took them to the stone ground. He remained silent. I was wearing nothing else, just my shoes.

When he didn't speak after a few moments, I pulled the straps of my stilettos and dropped them off of each foot and turned around.

Standing before him like this, with the slight breeze in my hair, I felt vulnerable. Anyone from the street could see through the iron gates. My neighbors could see me in the courtyard. But none of this seemed to matter, because what really made me blush and squirm was knowing that he was there. Right there, and he was seeing me. Seeing all of me.

I tried to cross my arms over my small breasts, but he took my hand gently and helped me over to where he'd parked his car.

Classical music played on his radio as I tried to find a comfortable spot on the leather. I worried about how aroused I was; I might stain his seat. He rested a hand on my thigh, stroking it absently, and whispered for me to keep still. As a reward for my obedience, he dragged his fingers over my clit, again and again. He outlined my opening, teasing each fold gently. He let his fingers slide into me and I lost control. I fell back against the seat, legs tense, arching my pelvis upward to make it easier for him to finger-fuck me.

He chuckled but indulged me, moving his fingers inside of me and curling them forward. I did most of the rest of the work as he drove. Shamelessly, I rode his thrusts on that seat, bringing my knees up onto the cushion so I could straddle his fingers and hold the top of the car.

We were at a stoplight when I came. At least, the car was stopped anyway. He could've been at a huge intersection with hundreds of people watching me this way. I'd stretched out over the seat, leaning on the dash with my head buried under my arms. I rocked against his fingers, twisting my hips to get him right where I wanted him. And I wanted him there. I wanted him to keep touching that spot. I could picture it—soft warmth around his cool hands, my body taking him, spreading open for him, engulfing his fingers as I whined and moaned and begged for more. I felt like I was going to sob before I finally came. He was expert at feeding me just a little until I thought I might go crazy or lose the feeling and then he'd start again, slowly, methodically.

I was loud when I came. I could feel how close the windshield was, but I couldn't hear anything but the soft music and my breathing. I wanted to leap into his lap and kiss him, to pull down his trousers and suck his cock. I was so aroused I didn't know what to do with myself, even after my orgasm. But he said, "Sit now. And wait."

It wasn't very long until we'd reached our destination. It felt like hours. Each time I reached to finger myself and relive what we'd just done, he took my hand and set it back on the console. When we finally arrived, I wasn't sure I could breathe from how badly I needed it.

But that was not to be. Not then.

I thought I heard a fountain and horses whinnying in the background. The grass I walked on was soft and lush, the cobbles uneven, rough. It was a suburb almost certainly, but maybe it was way out in the country.

I hadn't even told anyone I'd be gone.

The notion thrilled and frightened me, but I did nothing other than follow where his hand guided me into a room of some sort. He took me in a few more steps and then told me to put my hands down at my sides. I thought about asking what he was doing, but we'd come so far and I'd already come once. I couldn't imagine anything but a good time.

I'd never been tied up before, so I didn't know what to feel when he dragged his ropes over my body. They stung a little over my nipple but otherwise were surprisingly soft. I might have thought they were silk had he not said that they were his special hemp rope.

"I only use it for special occasions. It means much to me. You cannot buy rope like this. It has to be cured, burned on the outside and worked until it becomes soft like this. It has to be used, warmed and loved." Something about what he said quashed what little fear I had that he might be tying me up to kill me. He sounded so reverent about his ropes, and I couldn't help but feel honored that he wanted to introduce them to me.

He ran the ropes over my shoulders. It was like silk pressing along my spine, down my body. He curled the rope around a breast and then pulled it through between my legs. The rope pulled just so, reawakening whatever arousal I'd lost. I could feel the wet spot on the rope as he wound it over my body. It felt so peaceful, so relaxing to just have the rope winding around me. I didn't even notice when the rope started getting tighter, when it started to take on more thickness.

Slowly, I was being restricted. Rope was tied to rope and twisted around one part of my body and then tied over to another part. My hands could still move, so I felt the octagonal pattern around my belly button and reached down to feel a smartly tied knot of rope between my legs, just above the clit. At my discovery, he lightly pulled the rope and I felt such a gentle tugging everywhere, it made me shiver. The knot pressed against my clit, which made me moan and contort to feel it again. Ropes were bound around my small breasts, pushing all of the blood to my nipples, making them highly sensitive when John turned me around to run his tongue over them.

He always moved me, never moved around me. I was to go to him, never the other way around. His hands felt so light, his rope so strong, that soon I was completely immobilized. He bent me over, untying one section of the ropes only to secure them again behind me. Then I heard a small clatter from the tile floor. Something was being pulled toward me and again I felt that thrill of fear, the fear that something horrible might happen to me.

Instead, I heard what sounded like a ripcord and the snap of a latch. Then, slowly, I was rising up into the air. My feet left the ground and immediately I felt the hard tug of the ropes as I was suspended. The knot at my clit tightened, rubbed. The ropes massaged my breasts, held me in place, made me feel everything more keenly than I'd ever felt anything on my body.

The rope was soft, but firm, not biting into my skin, but not giving way. I was hanging from my whole body. It felt like I was flying.

I heard his zipper and the sound of clothes falling to the floor, then the snap of a condom.

His body was warm between my legs as he positioned himself behind me. I could feel the head of his prick teasing me, but I had no leverage to push back against it, to make him give me what I'd been dying for since we met. I curled my toes and fingers and whined, trying to shift my hips.

"You really want me, don't you?" His voice sounded amused, maybe a little surprised. "Do I scare you?"

"I should be scared, but I'm not. I want this. I want you. I want you to fuck me and then I want you to fuck me again." I was drooling with it, head bowed, hair flopping around my cheeks. My whole body felt hot with embarrassment for begging, but I needed it. My cunt was twitching, begging, tightening, grasping, trying anything for friction, for more of that perfection.

"I want you, too," he whispered. I felt every inch of him slowly sliding into me. I could take all of it, wanted to keep taking all of it until I was filled with him. I tried to grab on to anything I could for leverage to push against him, but I was powerless. I couldn't do it. Instead, I had to rely on him to move, to slide his cock just there. He read me well, knowing when to squeeze my thighs, when to thrust hard and when to let up. I knew that I could've told him no at any time during this. He would have stopped. But I was glad I hadn't, glad that I could give myself to him this way, which was more than I ever would've believed of myself.

Our bodies slapped together wetly, his hands on my hips to keep me moving. I could tell he was going to come by the noises he made, by the way he moved. I focused, working with him, thinking about his cock inside of me, about me floating above the ground somewhere I didn't even know. Somewhere that there could be people, quiet people, or maybe a video camera. I didn't know who could be looking at me like this and I didn't care. All I cared about was coming, about getting off.

I couldn't remember a time when I'd ever been fucked so hard or so thoroughly. His fingers bit into my flesh as he came and I came with him, my whole body vibrating. It felt like I was having a seizure, a complete out-of-body experience. I saw stars, blinding bright, saw him standing there in front of my apartment with what looked like an innocent black scarf. Thinking of him, I came.

ABOUT THE AUTHORS

JACQUELINE APPLEBEE (writing-in-shadows.co.uk) breaks down barriers with smut. Jacqueline's stories have appeared in various anthologies and websites, including Cleansheets, *Best Women's Erotica, Best Lesbian Erotica, Where the Girls Are*, and *Girl Crazy*.

M. CHRISTIAN has more than 300 stories in anthologies like *Best American Erotica, Best Gay Erotica, Best Lesbian Erotica*, and many other venues. He is the editor of twenty anthologies, and author of more than eight collections, including *Dirty Words, The Bachelor Machine, Filthy*, and the novels *Running Dry, The Very Bloody Marys, Me2, Brushes*, and *Painted Doll*.

ELIZABETH COLDWELL lives and writes in London. Her stories have appeared in a number of Cleis Press anthologies including *Bottoms Up, Spanked*, and *Please, Sir*, as well as books by numerous other publishers. She can be found online at The

(Really) Naughty Corner (elizabethcoldwell.wordpress.com).

MATT CONKLIN turns his perverted pursuits into erotic fiction whenever he has the chance. Look for his work in *The Mile High Club, He's on Top,* and other books.

Often based on her own explorations in the world of D/s and BDSM, **TESS DANESI** looks into the darker side of erotica, writing with raw honesty about that shadowy area where pain becomes pleasure and pleasure pain. Tess has been published in several anthologies edited by Alison Tyler and Rachel Kramer Bussel as well as in *Time Out New York*. She blogs about life, death, and everything in between at Urban Gypsy (nyc-urban-gypsy.blogspot.com).

AMANDA EARL's sexually explicit fiction has appeared in anthologies by Cleis Press, Alyson Books, Thunder's Mouth Press, and Carroll and Graf. Online, you can find her stories at Unlikelystories.org and Lies With Occasional Truth (lwot.net). For further information, please visit amandaearl.com.

JUSTINE ELYOT has written stories, long and short, for Cleis Press, Black Lace, and Total E-Bound, among others. Her most recent full-length book, *The Business of Pleasure*, was published by Xcite Press in September 2010. She likes the lightly romantic and the darkly erotic and vice versa.

EMERALD's erotic fiction has been published in anthologies edited by Violet Blue, Rachel Kramer Bussel, Jolie du Pre, and Alison Tyler as well as at various erotic websites. She lives in Maryland and serves as an activist for reproductive freedom and sex workers' rights. Find her online at thegreenlightdistrict.org.

SHANNA GERMAIN finds the smallest things sexy: tiny scars, far-away stars, and specks of dust. Her work has appeared in *Best American Erotica, Best Bondage Erotica, Best Gay Romance, Best Lesbian Erotica, Please, Sir,* and more. Visit her at www.shannagermain.com.

ISABELLE GRAY's writing appears in many anthologies.

NOELLE KEELY is the pseudonym of a widely-published writer of erotica and romance. She hopes the ancestors from whom she borrowed elements of her nom de plume are rolling over in their graves at her appearance in anthologies such as *She's on Top* and this one.

FIONA LOCKE is a very kinky girl. She feels there's simply nothing to compare with the warm glow of a smacked bottom. Her debut novel, *Over the Knee*, is a semi-autobiographical account of her fantasies and experiences in the spanking scene. The publisher even convinced her to pose for the cover.

LOLITA LOPEZ writes deliciously naughty romantic and erotic tales in various genres. When not writing, she's hanging out with her kiddo, loving on her husband, or chasing after their big, blubbering Great Dane, Bosley. You can find Lo's latest releases at lolitalopez.com.

GWEN MASTERS (gwenmasters.net) has seen hundreds of her short stories published in print and online, and her erotic novels have been translated into half a dozen different languages. When she's not writing smut, she is exploring the world with a camera, researching interesting yet obscure topics, hopping a plane every few weeks, and masquerading as a serious news journalist.

222

CLANCY NACHT squeezes writing in amongst her job, her husband, and three feral rescue cats. She has written erotic fiction since 2003 but did not delve into professional writing until 2009. Since then, she has been published by Cleis Press, Ravenous Romance, Noble Romance, and Dreamspinner Press.

Originally from England, **TERRI PRAY** (terripray.com) now lives in Minnesota with her husband and their two children. Her work ranges from the mild to the wild and spans eleven publishing companies, and 100 novels, novellas, and short stories in anthologies.

TERESA NOELLE ROBERTS writes romance for the horny and erotica for the romantic, with a special love for things kinky and/or paranormal. Her short fiction has appeared in numerous anthologies, including *Please Ma'am: Erotic Stories of Male Submission*, *The Mile High Club*, and *Passion: Erotic Romance for Women*. She's written several erotic romances for Samhain and Phaze.

THOMAS S. ROCHE's short stories have appeared in more than 200 anthologies, including the *Best American Erotica* series, the *Best New Erotica* series, and many other best-of anthologies. Though primarily known as a writer of erotic stories, he also writes horror, crime fiction and nonfiction, and maintains a blog at thomasroche.com.

DOMINIC SANTI (dominicsanti@yahoo.com) is a former technical editor turned rogue whose stories have appeared in many dozens of publications, including *Please, Ma'am; Caught Looking; Sex and Candy; Secret Slaves*; and *Red Hot Erotica*. Future plans include more dirty short stories and an even dirtier historical novel.

DONNA GEORGE STOREY would still be in school if she'd met a professor like Dr. Perkins. She is the author of *Amorous Woman*, a steamy tale of an American woman's love affair with Japan and has written too many stories about masterful men to list here, but stop by DonnaGeorgeStorey.com to read more.

ALISON TYLER's twenty-five naughty novels and fifty erotic anthologies have won her the title of "Erotica's Own Super Woman" (East Bay Literary Examiner). Her most recent anthology, *Alison's Wonderland*, was published by Harlequin Spice in July 2010. She serves coffee and snark 24/7 at alisontyler. blogspot.com.

ABOUT
THE EDITOR

RACHEL KRAMER BUSSEL (rachelkramerbussel.com) is a New York-based author, editor, and blogger. She has edited over thirty books of erotica, including *Best Bondage Erotica 2011; Gotta Have It; Orgasmic; Bottoms Up: Spanking Good Stories; Spanked; Naughty Spanking Stories from A to Z 1* and *2; Fast Girls; Smooth; Passion; The Mile High Club; Do Not Disturb; Tasting Him; Tasting Her; Please, Sir; Please, Ma'am; He's on Top; She's on Top; Caught Looking; Hide and Seek; Crossdressing;* and *Rubber Sex.* She is the author of the forthcoming novel, *Everything But..., Best Sex Writing* series editor, and winner of 5 IPPY (Independent Publisher) Awards. Her work has been published in over one hundred anthologies, including *Best American Erotica 2004* and *2006;* Zane's *Chocolate Flava 2* and *Purple Panties; Everything You Know About Sex Is Wrong; Single State of the Union;* and *Desire: Women Write About Wanting.* She serves as senior editor at *Penthouse Variation,* and wrote the popular "Lusty Lady" column for *The Village Voice.*

Rachel is a sex columnist for SexIsMagazine.com and has written for *AVN, Bust,* Cleansheets.com, *Cosmopolitan, Curve,* The Daily Beast, Fresh Yarn, TheFrisky.com, Gothamist, Huffington Post, Mediabistro, *Newsday, New York Post, Penthouse, Playgirl, Radar, San Francisco Chronicle, Time Out New York,* and *Zink,* among others. She has appeared on "The Martha Stewart Show," "The Berman and Berman Show," NY1, and Showtime's "Family Business." She has hosted In The Flesh Erotic Reading Series (inthefleshreadingseries.com) since October 2005, featuring readers from Susie Bright to Zane, about which the *New York Times*'s UrbanEye newsletter said, she "welcomes eroticism of all stripes, spots, and textures." She blogs at lustylady.blogspot.com. Read more about *Surrender* at hersurrender.wordpress.com.

PERMISSIONS

Erotica for Every Kink

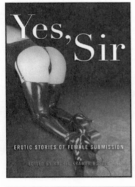

Yes, Sir
Erotic Stories of Female Submission
Edited by Rachel Kramer Bussel

The lucky women in *Yes, Sir* give up control to irresistibly powerful men who understand that dominance is about exulting in power that is freely yielded.
ISBN 978-1-57344-310-4 $15.95

Best Bondage Erotica
Edited by Alison Tyler

Always playful and dangerously explicit, these arresting fantasies grab you, tie you down, and never let you go.
ISBN 978-1-57344-173-5 $15.95

Best Bondage Erotica 2
Edited by Alison Tyler

From start to finish, these stories of women and men in the throes of pleasurable restraint will have you bound to your chair and begging for more!
ISBN 978-1-57344-214-5 $16.95

Spanked
Red Cheeked Erotica
Edited by Rachel Kramer Bussel

"Editrix extraordinaire Rachel Kramer Bussel has rounded up twenty brisk and stinging tales that reveal the many sides of spanking, from playful erotic accent to punishing payback for a long ago wrong."—Clean Sheets
ISBN 978-1-57344-319-7 $14.95

Rubber Sex
Edited by Rachel Kramer Bussel

Rachel Kramer Bussel showcases a world where skin gets slipped on tightly, then polished, stroked, and caressed—while the bodies inside heat up with lust.
ISBN 978-1-57344-313-5 $14.95

Ordering is easy! Call us toll free or fax us to place your MC/VISA order. You can also mail the order form below with payment to: Cleis Press, 2246 Sixth St., Berkeley, CA 94710.

ORDER FORM

QTY	TITLE	PRICE

SUBTOTAL _____

SHIPPING _____

SALES TAX _____

TOTAL _____

Add $3.95 postage/handling for the first book ordered and $1.00 for each additional book. Outside North America, please contact us for shipping rates. California residents add 9.75% sales tax. Payment in U.S. dollars only.

★ **Free book of equal or lesser value. Shipping and applicable sales tax extra.**

Cleis Press • Phone: (800) 780-2279 • Fax: 510-845-8001
orders@cleispress.com • www.cleispress.com
You'll find more great books on our website

Follow us on Twitter @cleispress • Friend/fan us on Facebook